HOW TO WRITE CRIME

HOW TO WRITE CRIME

edited by

Marele Day

ALLEN & UNWIN

First published in 1996 by
Allen & Unwin Pty Ltd
9 Atchison Street, St Leonards, NSW 2065 Australia

National Library of Australia
Cataloguing-in-Publication entry:

How to write crime.

ISBN 1 86373 998 X.

1. Detective and mystery stories—Authorship. I. Day,
Marele

808.3872

Set in 11/12.5pt NewBaskerville by DOCUPRO, Sydney
Printed by McPherson's Printing Group, Maryborough, Victoria

10 9 8 7 6 5 4 3 2 1

CONTENTS

CONTRIBUTORS

Debra Adelaide is a writer and freelance editor. She has published several books on Australian women writers and is the author of two crime fictions (one written in collaboration and published in 1993, the other, *The Life of Riley*, unpublished). Her other books include the novel *The Hotel Albatross* (Random House, 1995) and the anthology *Motherlove: births, babies and beyond* (ed. Random House, 1996). She is working on a historical narrative and more crime fiction.

Jean Bedford was born in England in 1946 and came to Australia in 1947. She has been a journalist, a publisher's editor, a teacher of English as a Second Language and of Creative Writing. She has published nine works of fiction, including three detective novels featuring private eye Anna Southwood. She is married to Peter Corris and now lives full-time on the Illawarra coast of New South Wales.

J.R. Carroll was born in 1945 and studied English and History at Melbourne University. He was a teacher for a number of years before turning to full-time writing in the late 1980s.

His first novel, *Token Soldiers*, was published in 1983. This was followed by *Catspaw* (1988), *Tropic of Fear* (1990), *No Way*

Back (1992), its sequel *Out of the Blue* (1993), and *Stingray* (1994). He reviews thrillers for *The Age*, and is the regular crime reviewer for the *Australian Book Review*.

J.R. Carroll lives with his wife in inner-suburban Melbourne. His interests include travel, film, fishing and Asian cuisine.

Stuart Coupe has been reading crime, mystery and detective fiction since he discovered Enid Blyton's Famous Five books. He is the editor and co-publisher of *Mean Streets* magazine and a regular crime fiction reviewer for the *Sydney Morning Herald* and the *Sunday Age*. With Julie Ogden, he has edited three anthologies of crime fiction; *Hardboiled, Case Reopened* and *Crosstown Traffic* (also edited by Robert Hood). He is completing a biography of Peter Corris that is only a couple of years behind schedule.

Marele Day grew up in Sydney and graduated from Sydney University with BA (Hons). Now a full-time writer, her work experience ranges from fruit picking to academic teaching. She has travelled extensively and lived in Italy, France and Ireland. Travels include a voyage by yacht from Cairns to Singapore which resulted in near shipwreck in the Java Sea. *The Life and Crimes of Harry Lavender* was her first thriller, published by Allen & Unwin in 1988. This was followed in 1990 by *The Case of the Chinese Boxes* and *The Last Tango of Dolores Delgado* in 1992 which won the 1993 Shamus Crime Fiction Award. *The Disappearances of Madalena Grimaldi*, the latest Claudia Valentine thriller, was published in 1994.

Garry Disher grew up in rural South Australia and now lives near the Victorian coast. In 1978 he attended Stanford University, in California, on a creative writing fellowship, and on his return to Australia supplemented his writing income by teaching fiction writing for a number of years. During that time he wrote several books, including the writers' handbooks *Writing Fiction* and *Writing Professionally*. A full-time writer since 1988, he is the author of award-winning novels, short-story collections, textbooks, anthologies and children's books. His crime fiction includes numerous stories and the Wyatt novels *Kickback, Paydirt, Deathdeal, Crosskill* and *Port Vila Blues.*

Kerry Greenwood has written a number of plays and has worked as a folk singer, a factory hand, a director, a producer, a translator, a costume maker, a cook, and also qualified as a solicitor. She is currently working on her eighth Phryne Fisher book, *Urn Burial;* a book of essays on female murderers called *The Thing She Loves;* a cookbook-and-detective-story pastiche called *Recipes for Crime* with Dr Jenny Pausacker (McPhee Gribble, November 1995); and *Cassandra,* a historical novel (Heinemann, September 1995). She is not married, has no children and lives with a registered wizard.

Sandra Harvey has written three books about notorious Australian murders. *Brothers in Arms* (Allen & Unwin, 1989); *My Husband, My Killer* (Allen & Unwin, 1992); *The Killer Next Door* (Random House, 1994). A Sydney newspaper crime and police reporter for twelve years, she is currently seeing things from the other side working as a press secretary to the NSW Minister for Police.

When she is not writing speeches, attending police graduations or tagging along to police station openings, she toys with other book ideas (more murder, of course), reads, listens to music and draws daily inspiration from the ocean floor at Coogee where she swims most mornings.

Stephen Knight has written a book, many articles and (for *The Sydney Morning Herald*) regular reviews on crime fiction; he also edited the first four of the 'Crimes for a Summer Christmas' series with Allen & Unwin. For many years he taught English at the Universities of Sydney and Melbourne and is now Professor and Head of School at the University of Wales, Cardiff.

Nigel Krauth teaches writing at Griffith University Gold Coast. His forays into the crime genre include the novella 'Worry No More' in the Coupe and Ogden collection *Case Reopened* (Allen & Unwin, 1993).

Robert Wallace's first Essington Holt novel appeared in England in 1988. Essington is a rich layabout whose interests include art forgery and sexual politics (at which he's a dud.) Other books are *Payday*, *Flood Rain* and *Art Rat*. Robert Wallace lives in the Southern Tablelands of New South Wales, with dogs and some retired stockhorses, where he relaxes a lot and paints beautiful pictures.

Minette Walters, a former journalist and editor, is the author of *The Ice House*, *The Sculptress*, *The Scold's Bridle*, and *The Dark Room*. She lives in Hampshire, England, with her husband and two sons, and is working on her fifth novel.

INTRODUCTION

Marele Day

There's a Monty Python sketch that goes something like this:

> Good morning, boys and girls. Today we are going to learn to play the flute. Are you all sitting comfortably? Good. To play the flute you just pick up the instrument, put your fingers over the holes and blow. Easy, isn't it? Tomorrow we are going to learn how to do brain surgery.

How do you write a crime novel? The short answer is you just sit down, put your fingers on the keyboard and type till the story comes out. The long answer (or answers) would fill a book. On the one hand, writing is a matter of sitting down and tapping the keys till you've got a few hundred pages worth of story. But that doesn't adequately explain what's happening while you are seated—the creation of characters, the working out of the plot, the writing of gripping action scenes, the unobtrusive planting of clues, the way you blend the real with the imagined to make a plausible story.

There are things that only you can bring to the writing process—tenacity, discipline, motivation and that quality that we recognise as soon as we see it but find so hard to define—talent. Reading this book and doing the exercises is not a guarantee that you will automatically turn into a published writer. But it can show you skills, techniques and short cuts; offer ways of solving problems. Most importantly, it provides maps drawn by those who have already explored the terrain. A map is something you consult before you embark on a journey to give you an idea of where you're going. It can also be used as a reference as you go along, if you are lost and need to get back on the track. But you don't have to blindly, slavishly follow it. If you have your eye on the map all the time you miss the scenery. Once you're on the road you may find new paths and make your own map.

Crime fiction writers are storytellers. They give you the thrill of the new and the comfort of the old. Crime fiction readers have certain expectations. They expect a crime to be committed and that during the course of the story the writer will supply the answers to the questions surrounding the crime—the how-why-who-where-and-when of it. That's the comfort of the old. The thrill of the new is how-why-who-where-and-when the writer fulfils those expectations. There are rules but they can be bent or broken. Each new writer adds to the genre and changes its shapes. While crime fiction never loses sight of the fact that it is telling stories, it has its eye, private or public, on the real world. It is about people and places, real or thinly disguised. Its eye is a camera recording every little detail of our lives, the sleaze and the glamour, as night closes in on the twentieth century. With crime fiction we enter zones we are reluctant to venture into on our own but which nevertheless intrigue—ill-lit streets, the mysterious underworld, the dark places of the heart.

The contributors to this book represent a whole range of crime writing—true crime, private eye, tough guy, historical thriller, psychothriller. All alive and doing very well. Crime fiction relies on Darwinian principles of survival—diversity in the species and the ability to adapt to the environment. The story can be dressed up in many ways, but it always talks to us in the language of our time and place.

This book was conceived as a practical 'how to' guide on writing crime fiction. I invited each contributor to focus on a specific aspect of the craft—research, plot and structure, character, dialogue, style, editing and so on. But then, as they say, 'the plot thickened'. It thickened in a couple of ways. It is impossible to pull out these strands and examine them separately without considering them in relation to the whole work and inevitably the different sections overlap. But rather than being simply repetitive, the resonance gives depth and dimension. Ideas that are seeded in one chapter are developed in another. Some are contradicted, providing a different point of view and showing that there's more than one way of going about it. It is as if crime writing were a baton each writer picked up, ran with for their lap and then passed on to the next writer.

Journalist and true-crime writer Sandra Harvey shows us how to track down the nitty-gritty details that lend your work solidity and authenticity. Then Kerry Greenwood puts her fictional creation Phryne Fisher onto the stage of real-life Melbourne in the 1920s. Garry Disher takes the skeleton out of the closet and shows us how to assemble the plot, the bones of any good crime story. Minette Walters talks of character and plays the 'what if?' game with John, Michael, Mary and Hannah. And J.R. Carroll lets his characters do the talking in the chapter on dialogue. Debra Adelaide gives us a stylish piece on style and plays with the clichés of crime fiction. Robert Wallace writes entertainingly of beginnings, endings and bits in between. Nigel Krauth steps into the twin roles of writer and private eye in his persuasive piece on setting, action and suspense—I was almost convinced we really did have all those fictional phone calls. Jean Bedford takes you gently but firmly by the hand and guides you through the whole process from rough idea to final draft. And my chapter, 'Taking Care of Business', gives you some clues as to what you can do once the manuscript is finished. The ensemble is bracketed with pieces from our commentators: Stephen Knight, who offers an enlightening chapter on genre and subgenre, what's been done with them in the past and what may be done with them in the future; and Stuart Coupe, reader extraordinaire, knows a good story when he sees one and keeps on looking.

The other way the plot thickened was that the book became much more than a practical guide. It reveals writers at work— the way they approach what they do—as well as giving us valuable insights into how their books were produced. Knowing how particular novels were put together makes you want to go back and read the author's work afresh. It is obvious that some contributors had fun writing their piece. Others said they found it instructive to think about how they do what they do. Because you can write a good crime story doesn't necessarily mean you have the ability to analyse and articulate the process. The contributors to this book do reveal how they do it, and, whether you want to write a story of your own or whether you're simply a reader interested in crime writing, the various pieces will entertain and inform you.

Guidelines, rules, processes, maps. You can follow all the instructions but that won't give the breath of life to the story. The breath of life comes from somewhere else. It comes from playing. Play is important when you're making something out of nothing, which is what fiction writers do. Play is uncritical, it is adventurous, it tries out ideas, it experiments. Play is full of possibilities, it is not afraid to take a punt. It asks 'What if?' Play is the other side of writing, the side that is invisible. This is the 'work' done while you're lying on the couch daydreaming. Conjure up your fictional world and wander around in it. Throw ideas up in the air and see where they land.

There's a time for being critical, for rigorously appraising your work, but it's not at the beginning. For the moment, ignore the raven of doubt sitting on your shoulder. You are starting with the rough idea, not the polished story that this idea will eventually become. Get something down on paper. It doesn't have to come out right first go. No-one ever wrote straight off the book that ended up in the bookstore. As Ernest Hemingway said to F. Scott Fitzgerald: 'I write a page of masterpiece to 99 pages of shit.' If a thing's worth doing it's worth doing badly at first, then fixing up.

Lastly, stop *wanting* to write a crime story. Go to the desk and start *writing*. Stop cleaning the fridge, stop sharpening the pencils and arranging the furniture. Start. Just sit down, put your fingers on the keys and type.

Marele Day
Sydney, 1995

1 WHAT KIND OF GHOUL AM I? GENRE AND SUBGENRE

Stephen Knight

Towards genre

Genre is one of those words which, by virtue of being hard to pronounce or spell, or just by looking strange, don't seem to belong to English properly, and as a result people rarely like to think about what they mean. Syntax is another of those words: even those who study linguistics seem to veer away from this strange-looking term.

But the things these words represent are with us all the time; we structure everything we say in syntax, and we cannot speak or write without selecting a genre, without adopting a kind of communication which has certain rules and expectations.

Our innate knowledge of genre is indicated by the fact that it is so easily signalled. If the camera catches the down-turned brim of a trilby hat and a thin spiral of smoke passing it, we know where we are—1940s America; and we know in detail the attitudes and even the lighting that will follow—noir to a degree. Equally, if the opening scene of the novel describes a wry, youngish woman gazing irritably around her less than suave apartment, we are headed almost certainly for a feminist thriller.

These cues seem automatic for us as consumers of crime fiction. Yet for the creator they depend on generic choices— private eye rather than adventure story, feminist thriller rather than clue puzzle. The aspiring crime writer will, by the language, characters, settings, crimes, detection methods that he or she chooses, construct a particular genre. Success, sales, even immortality, may depend on that choice.

It may not be a simple choice, or an immediate one. Nor, perhaps, should it be. If you are absolutely certain how you want to write, then consider whether in fact you are not too firmly under the influence of someone who has already done it better. Many major authors only slowly developed the form in which they write best and for which they are best known. Raymond Chandler, lord of the tough-guy writers, started his career by synopsising the plots of a writer so far from male excitement as Erle Stanley Gardner, creator of the Perry Mason courtroom dramas, and the early Raymond Chandler stories (*Killer in the Rain* is a good collection) are without the prose poetry and the suffering sensitivity that made Philip Marlowe so popular.

Agatha Christie may seem the most automatically facile author of the clever clue puzzle, but in her early days she alternated puzzles of precocious technique (*The Mysterious Affair at Styles* is a remarkable first novel) with thin and pompous spy stories. They reached their best, if that is the word, in *The Secret of Chimneys*, but they must be very disappointing to the many who still buy them in the uniform edition.

If even Christie was slow to see her best form, others may expect to move slowly to theirs. But it will still help to make thoughtful choices in terms of your own skills and knowledge, rather than make a pale copy of another writer's carefully developed pattern.

Naming the genre

Before getting down to investigative complexity, it is wise to make sure the terms and techniques are clear. A surprising amount of unclarity in writing on crime fiction comes from the overlapping terms that are used for the form.

Some call the genre itself the thriller, making much of the emotive impact on the reader; others like to call it the mystery, stressing the complexity of the plot. Detective story is also a favourite, focusing on the person who solves it all. Yet there are successful examples of crime fiction that lack any thrills (like Dennis Wheatley's police procedural files, literally files, not novels), there are some that lack mystery (like Francis Iles's breakthrough whydunits, which name the murderer in the first lines), and plenty lack detectives either amateur or professional (including Christie's own favourites *Towards Zero* and *Endless Night*). All of those terms are less than inclusive, but there are no examples of a genre without a crime or at least (as in Sir Arthur Conan Doyle's 'The Yellow Face') the appearance of a crime. So crime fiction, a term that may seem a little unexciting, but is accurately descriptive, remains by far the best name for the genre.

The other names that are sometimes given usually describe in fact a subgenre, and this is really the choice that the new writer makes. A lot of the subgeneric names identify a form through its techniques—police procedural à la Ed McBain, or 'clue puzzle', as done to a turn by the great women writers of the 'golden age', Christie, Dorothy Sayers, Margery Allingham, Ngaio Marsh (many would add Gladys Mitchell as well as a few men, especially John Dickson Carr). Other subgenres are named for an attitude which reacts against existing structures—tough guy fiction (also known more technically as private eye); feminist thrillers, as in the Sara Paretsky tradition; historical thrillers, with Ellis Peters in the undisputed lead. Then in some areas the existence of a subgenre is a matter for dispute. Is there a form called the psychothriller, as found in Patricia Highsmith, Ruth Rendell, Margaret Yorke, Minette Walters? I think this is in fact a separate subgenre because it is structurally identifiable: there is no formal detective-type investigation of the central threat, which is usually a fear of attack, or madness, or both. Less certainly, are we now seeing the emergence of a new subgenre in the thriller of violence, where the main feature is physical destruction, as in Thomas

Harris's novels, and where true crime journalism has some supporting role?

Versions of the genre

Among all of these forms, as well as many which are half and half (Harris's *Silence of the Lambs* is both a police procedural and a feminist thriller), the new writer must choose. And Australian writers are not without precedents to follow. Though people are increasingly aware of the strength of modern Australian crime writing, it has a history in most of the subgenres—Margot Neville was a fine clue puzzler, Pat Flower was good in that line and also, in her later novels, produced some excellent psychothrillers. Martin Long writes Sydney-based historical mysteries. The feminists are very well represented among Marele Day, Claire McNab, Jean Bedford and Kerry Greenwood. Jon Cleary writes fine police procedurals and Peter Corris is local king of the tough guy kids.

In fact there are subgenres which seem to be particularly strong in Australia. Other countries have felt no need of a name for the story that is written from a criminal's viewpoint and shows the law to be a pretty oppressive affair. Although Donald Westlake wrote several such novels as Richard Stark and Hollywood liked the pattern, especially in films starring Humphrey Bogart, it's only when you look at Australian crime fiction that you see many examples, past and present, from Marcus Clarke's *For the Term of His Natural Life* to Garry Disher's recent Wyatt series.

If a certain interest in the criminal's point of view might seem comprehensible in terms of Australian history, so might this country's other special subgenre, the nature detective story in which, by the end of what is basically a rural thriller without a detective, the criminal is destroyed by the forces of nature. The usual environmental avengers are fire, flood or mountain range, or even, in one of Beatrice Grimshaw's more startling stories, cannibals.

From exotic to familiar, the subgenres of crime fiction offer themselves to the aspiring writer. Partly the choice should be made in terms of what you know: it's unwise to get too much wrong. But it's also very important that you choose a subgenre where the form will work in itself as part of the values which you as the author offer as a way to control crime—at least in fiction.

For example, the clue puzzle marshals intellect alone as a mythic defence against crime. It is when we know who has 'done it' that the threat disappears. But in the noir tough guy story, a sense of knowing endurance is communicated as the true protection of the peaceful mind. The feminist thriller speaks about a sense of self-sufficiency as a protective force, and is as concerned about its defence of the female self as it is with preventing the heroine from being shot and beaten— notice how she seems always to have near at hand a senior but weak male to be both sympathetic and surpassed.

The subgenre, that is, needs to be part of the mechanism of fictional order which the text sets against the disorders that are imagined. The author should be committed to the values embodied in the genre itself: the police procedural is well written by those who value rational, patient, painful progress as a bulwark against omnipresent chaos; the psychothriller may belong to an opposite ideology, espoused by those who want to test the limits and indeed the depths of human capacity and courage in a tight and frightening place. The writer needs to think through the emotive meaning of the subgenre and opt for the one in which he or she feels potentially most at home, and so most alarmed by disruption.

Genre writing is often regarded as simple, like painting by numbers. But genres are misunderstood as mere sets of rules. True, they can be described in terms of rules, because they follow certain familiar patterns. But that is caused by the presence of a consistent pattern of response, not through external regulation. Genres are like clichés—they might seem hackneyed, but that is because they have recurrent value for many people over time. In terms of crime fiction, an anecdote might clarify the matter.

Some years ago I had the pleasure of meeting and inter-viewing Alan G. Yates, the English-born Sydney resident who, under the name Carter Brown, wrote best-selling crime fiction—128-page novellas focused on a private eye or a police lieutenant, mostly set in the US and almost always dripping with *Playboy*-type girls, Chandleresque plots of a complicated rather than complex kind, and, my favourite bit and no doubt most enjoyed by his adolescent audience in those innocent days, lots of elaborate evening meals. Pheasant under glass was often the real climax of interpersonal manoeuvres.

Alan was a bit late for lunch the day we were to do the interview. This was most unlike him, a very courteous and punctilious man. He was a little breathless, and apologised; he had slept in very late, he said, because the previous night he had cracked the problem of a book that was giving him difficulties. He'd been blocked for days on its ending, and then last night it had just come, and he had written the final six chapters in one sequence till 5 a.m.

Fascinating, I said. It was even more so when I bought the book to have a look at the ending. Like most of his, it had a peepshow title, *Blondes are Busting Out* or *Dames are Deadly*, that kind of thing. Equally familiar was the ending. The last six chapters, on which he had laboured to the point of lateness, were simply vintage Carter Brown generic cliché.

But, and the point is worth dwelling on, especially if you reflect on his huge sales, Alan did not do this by following rules. He reworked his subgenre every time; his technique was, as it were, reinvented every 128 pages. That commitment, and that continued vitality, is what the genre writer requires, and selecting the appropriate subgenre is a crucial step in enabling you as author to work in that way.

Locating the genre

A defining feature of the crime story is the place where it occurs. Making this choice may be the main step in choosing a subgenre, especially today, when there is a host of practices and patterns to guide expectations. If you want to write about a rain-swept town in northern England, then a police procedural may be the only viable form. If though, the corrupt streets of a Southeast Asian capital attract you, then a down-at-heel private eye may be the only proper vehicle.

A choice of place might seem to some a casual element in the construction of your pattern of writing, but it may well have deeper significance; it appears that place and its implications were a central feature in the establishment of the genre itself.

Commentators date the full development of the genre from the mid nineteenth century, especially when Edgar Allan Poe wrote his three famous stories starring the brilliant amateur detective Chevalier C. Auguste Dupin, he who solved the dreadful Murders in the Rue Morgue. There had been earlier fictional detectives, even in America, but none had been presented with such flair or such influence.

The keys to this were twofold. The crimes took place in a city, and a specially skilled individual was needed to detect them. These two facts are intimately connected: they are the basis for all modern crime fiction, including the varieties which deliberately move away from city and the individual detective. Earlier crime fiction—and there was plenty of it— was just as often set in the country, and most importantly did not rely on a detective. In the Newgate Calendar, for example, that rich source of criminal stories from the eighteenth century and earlier, crimes are solved in one of two ways. Someone sees the criminal in the act, or spots him, sometimes her, with the stolen money or with bloodstained hands. If that doesn't happen, the criminal is suddenly transfixed by guilt and a sense of having sinned against God's order. These social or religious systems of preventing crime made sense in communities where social bonds were recognised as powerful and where Christianity dominated everyday values.

But in the emergent cities, anonymity was normal, people could never know everyone they saw; and the rise of secular, mercantile values made Christianity's influence much less powerful. This was the real functional origin of crime fiction, in the need of a specialist character to identify the criminal. It is often said that there is detection in the Bible (the Esau–Jacob substitution trick) and in the classics (the case of Oedipus' father). This idea derives from Dorothy Sayers, who, in writing the introductions to her annual anthologies of the best in crime short stories, also set herself to give mystery writing an ancient authority. Like her other work, these introductions are memorable, brilliant. But unlike in her stories, the argument was forced. Those examples from the past were riddles, puzzles, enigmas, and culture has always enjoyed those in light or heavy form. But they never had a separate generic form, an identifiable niche in the marketplace like the yellow-covered novels that shrieked their genre from the railway bookstalls, or the green-and-white Penguins that in time of nuclear threat let you relax with a different and much more manageable kind of anxiety.

Crime fiction is a genre with an origin in the development of urban society. In the cities, the detective was born to defend against some of the most alarming features of this new civilisation, and the early stories are full of questions of identity, threats about the darkness of the modern heart. And intriguingly there is embodied in them an idea of movement, of the very newness of the city to the individual writer and reader; that the writer is a stranger to the location is often part of the dynamic effect, and you as author might well consider this when choosing your structure.

Poe, for example, wrote about Paris, but the stories appeared in his native American magazines. Conan Doyle, who shaped the myth of late Victorian London, was an Edinburgh man. Fergus Hume, whose *The Mystery of a Hansom Cab* made Melbourne the setting in 1886 of the first international bestseller in the genre, was brought up in New Zealand. The pattern continues today: in almost all cases the place chosen by a successful crime writer is one he or she knows with a fresh, surprised, even alarmed eye. Christie did not grow up in either a rural mansion or a sweet little village, nor yet a Mayfair flat—the varied settings of her best books. Though the city and its surprises are basic to much crime fiction, she showed there can be (as Doyle had indicated) a version wherein the countryside itself is threatening, in some ways more so than the criminals who inhabit it. Arthur Upfield, the best-selling author of tourist thrillers set in Australia, came from the green fields of Hampshire.

There may also be some crucial relationship between place and subgenre. Just as the tough guy story grew up in the streets of the American West, so other places and other forms may have strong links. Lisa Cody's realistic adventures of Anna Lee fit very well into seedy west London and might have been strangely distorted if set in a Yorkshire village. Presumably for historical reasons, police stories seem not to work well in Sydney, apart from Cleary's, and private eye dramas appear out of place in Melbourne. Perhaps the tough guy requires the Pacific, and proceduralism a less glaring light.

The same sense of appropriateness occurs in other locations. There is no doubt that an exotic setting can be good for marketing, but if it is merely backdrop the effect will soon seem thin. Tony Hillerman's powerful stories about crime in the Navajo context combine a breathtaking physical setting with a serious and quite passionate account of issues within American Indian communities. Frank Parrish's unusual West Country fables focusing on Dan Malet, poacher and detective, are ironically rich with anti-urban values, not just quaint pieces of poker-work rusticity.

So place should be known, but not known too comfortably, and most importantly known in terms of dynamic values and problems. The edge of anxiety and the possibility of resolution should be communicable in terms of location itself.

Peopling the genre

The patterns associated with place are broadly repeated in terms of character. A choice of personnel might itself precede and predetermine the subgenre. You might, for example, be an academic ironist absolutely determined to create a modern female version of Sherlock Holmes: clever, cavalier, a bit eccentric. That decision would almost certainly lead you to a version of the deductive detective, though probably a more active one than derives from the Hercule Poirot mould.

Or if you are interested in history, you might select a strong-minded woman operating in Gold Rush Melbourne (having read Mary Fortune and Randolph Bedford for preparation). This choice might push you towards the historical procedural, whose precedents include Baroness Orczy's Lady Molly stories and, more elusive yet (at least until my own forthcoming anthology), Andrew Forrester's *Tales of a Lady Detective* from as early as 1862.

If you have already settled on a subgenre then to some degree the character will be moulded by this choice: you can hardly have a procedural starring an eccentric amateur, though the idea might partly work (Nero Wolfe, through his assistant, is in some way an example); and you could hardly have a feminist thriller with a male cop as the star—though there might be one around for various purposes, as in Paretsky.

But even within the expectations of a subgenre there is usually still a fair bit of room to manoeuvre. Indeed, it may be the choice of detective character—if there is one—which in itself helps you settle on a version of the form. Some facts about international variation might be helpful here. Recently I did a survey of several hundred well-known crime novels to see how the types of detecting split up. I sorted them in terms of the basic type of detective method: police, private eye, amateur and—the most interesting category in many ways— zero detection, in which the characters themselves somehow discover, usually by accident, what has happened to them, or even where some force like fate or bad luck just frustrates the criminal's intention.

The results came out like this:

| Country | Detective method | | | |
	Police	Private eye	Amateur	Zero
UK	38%	7%	46%	9%
US	13%	50%	20%	17%
Australia	31%	25%	9%	35%

The figures imply some differing national ideas about what is the most credible form of fictional protection from disorder; who do people most believe in as a detective? They might also be read with an eye to sales for a particular form of subgenre— you're going to be uphill in Britain with a tough guy hero, and your gentleman amateur isn't going to cut much marketing ice in Australia.

But as with most statistics, these contain some complexities that need comment. They are, for instance, compiled from books published over a lengthy period, back to the mid nineteenth century. This range has a particularly strong effect on the Australian figures. It's often said that you can't get modern Australians to sympathise with police unless they are basically Irish and against the system like Cleary's Scobie Malone, or oppositive to it by virtue of being, say, a professional woman, or indeed a lesbian, like Claire McNab's Carol Ashton. But this is a relatively recent position. In the pages of the *Australian Journal*, that rich source of local crime fiction from the 1860s on, there are plenty of police detectives in city and bush. Dislike of the law seems to have been an offshoot of the development of the myth of the bushman: in the early stories escaped convicts or unreformed old lags are more of a threat than the cops.

Equally, the substantial number of private eyes found in Australian crime fiction are almost all very recent: most appeared in the 1980s in the wake of Peter Corris's Cliff Hardy and Marele Day's Claudia Valentine, but some other authors, like Otto Beeby and Ian Hamilton, can be traced back to the influx of American culture in the postwar period.

But if both the policeman and the private eye can be seen a little differently than those figures at first suggest, there is no doubting or redefining Australians' deep suspicion of the gentleman amateur. Indeed, a number of the police appear in the work of writers like Margot Neville or the early Pat Flower, who were really using the Christie–Sayers model but were not attracted to an amateur, and so created an intelligent and rather individualistic police detective to do the job instead.

Most striking of all, and a further sign, it would seem, of some deep strain of anti-authoritarianism in the Australian response to fictional crime, is the great weight given only in this country to zero detection. This runs right through the tradition; many of Mary Fortune's early stories lack a detective; the pattern is still found in the *Australian Journal* in the 1950s, and it is highlighted in the psychically focused drama of Pat Flower's later books and the criminal-centred ironic fatalism of Garry Disher's recent work.

To opt for zero detection is to suggest that no one type of person is seen as a credible agent of order in such a disorderly world. The quasi-science of Dupin and Holmes, the calm village wisdom of Miss Marple, the learning-backed insights of Lord Peter Wimsey, the strained integrity of Sam Spade, the relaxed but real fidelity of Cliff Hardy, the bravura heroism of Phryne Fisher, the stylish commitment of Claudia Valentine—on occasions none of these virtues, or their many other variants, create the inner core of confidence for author and reader that make the detective-based subgenres work.

Of course, zero detection makes the crime story much more like a conventional novel—*Emma* is one of the great zero detection mysteries, and could be subtitled 'The Case of the Mysterious Piano'. *Murder in the Cathedral* can be read as a historical whydunit. Going without a detective makes plotting and revelation more complex: you can't have the cosy scene where Hercule Poirot tells all, though that convention can itself lead to clumsiness. The zero detection story also looks towards the most modern fiction, in which the characters are absences or mysteries, as in Paul Auster's trilogy about strange presences and traces in New York and Jan McKemmish's fine piece of local postmodernism *A Gap in the Records*. Zero detection is popular, especially in Australia, and as a new author you might therefore take it seriously as an option. But it's not easy to bring off; and national dignity would benefit from the avoidance of more tourist tales in which the villain just happens to be eaten by a giant crocodile.

Crimes and methods of detection

When you have assembled the place and the people that bring to life the crime genre, there has to be something to be detected. Another defining feature of the crime story, and a crucial range of choice for the aspiring author, is not who, where or why, but what was actually done. Crimes can vary as much as the rest of the elements in the thriller.

This is sometimes a surprise to those who think of the genre as dealing exclusively with death. *Bloody Murder* was the title

Julian Symons used for his survey of the field, and though in the US this was regarded as too strong a phrase, its euphemism had the same fatal message—*Mortal Consequences*. However, in the past the crime that focused the anxiety of the readers was not always, indeed not often, murder. It's one of the intriguing questions about the form in general: Why did the twentieth century became so obsessed with death?

Sherlock Holmes himself observes that most of his early cases (those appearing in *The Adventures of Sherlock Holmes* and the *Memoirs* that followed it) were not based on violent crime but often on theft or even simply on trickery of some kind, as in 'A Case of Identity', the second story of all, in which a father has been impersonating his daughter's fiancé. Much more interesting than murder, especially when you think that Dr Freud was busily at work in another European metropolis at just the same time as Dr Conan Doyle.

It's a legitimate consideration for the new author: Do you have to have a killing? Might we not by now be ready for thrillers dealing with other kinds of crime, driving someone mad, for example, or stealing from a pension fund? What about, in our increasingly qualification-obsessed days, fraud in the professions, or the financial peccadilloes that can, if uncovered, destroy a fine career? It would be easy to seem original while being in fact very old fashioned and showing the horror that lurks in everyday malpractice—it's one of the elements in the psychothriller, especially as Margaret Yorke creates it, to focus on minor strains that can seem enormous. Though she does usually add a murder, no doubt with a view to publishers' expectations, it is often not central to the effect and structure of her work.

Given modern expectations, however, most writers will use murder as at least a part of the central plotting. Decisions of course arise about how it is presented. Death can be almost benign in the classic clue puzzles, where the body is just a little slumped and the tasteful oriental dagger hardly disturbs the cut across the shoulders of the squire's jacket. None of the rictus or stench of death there. Nowadays, the novel is more likely to open with every vivid detail of the outraged body, especially the lacerated flesh of a young female. But however you decide to shape them, tone and emotive attitude are set from the start, and will for success need to be consistent, which will usually mean uniform. It's hard to be brutally realistic and also poetically insightful, unless your name is Raymond Chandler; it's even harder to be reticent about what has happened and also harshly truth telling, unless your name is Patricia Highsmith. The means of presentation, even the type of language used, participate in a major way in the credibility of the fiction, and are also part of the value system which is ratified in the resolution of the crime.

Much of Christie's strength as a restorer of normal and conservative order comes through the heavily normative, almost cliché-ridden nature of her prose. Simple and clear—her books are widely used by learners of English—her style portrays a world where truths are also simple and clear, where evil people commit murder and truly good people, if a bit eccentric-seeming, are our best defences against such horror. The more complex kinds of analysis offered by, say, Ruth Rendell writing as the hall-of-mirrors expert Barbara Vine, or by Elmore Leonard in his obliquely hip way, are realised in styles of prose and scene setting that are never simple or static, but keep displacing certainties and deferring convictions of all kinds.

A central element in this construction of value in such fiction is the ways in which the crime is detected, the systems for restoring order that the fiction offers. Apart from the primary choice of subgenre, setting and type of detective, there is also the highly emphasised question of investigative technique—indeed, this is what essentially distinguishes one subgenre from another. The term clue puzzle identified the highly exotic system perfected by Christie, but already in place in Poe, whereby the reader, as well as the detective, can solve the mystery by induction (deduction is actually the wrong word because it means finding a preexisting law; it's a new and so truly revealing pattern you find in the baffling data). Intellectual analysis is privileged by the clue puzzle; many a bookish person has felt consoled by the trick.

Equally, the tough guy learns what has happened simply by exercising toughness—both of skull and, as Sam Spade shows, of heart. He turns in Miss Wonderly in spite of thinking she is wonderful. The private eye in fact uses his eyes to detect hardly at all, he just watches others with suspicious envious fear for the most part, with a little lust thrown in.

What the detective does—or, in the case of zero-detection plots, doesn't do—will shape the responses to crime that are felt to be most credible by writer and reader. But there is a surprise here. For some reason (another case for Freud, no doubt), the detectives who are most credible are themselves always partly criminal or capable of becoming a criminal. It makes sense, of course. The original police were reformed criminals, and today the best thief catcher is always close to the criminals: as is the case with spies, it's not always clear who is on whose side.

Sherlock Holmes is the good reflex of Professor Moriarty; Poirot sees and comprehends all, especially the darkness of the murderer's heart. The private eye has usually left the police under a cloud of some kind. Even Sara Paretsky's V.I. Warshawski, the St Joan of designer detection, has a coldly focused side to her that fires her determination enough to bring about her triumph.

The key point is that in crime fiction as in all literature, too perfect a figure is of little attraction to the average person. When Tennyson made Sir Galahad say 'My strength is as the strength of ten/ Because my heart is pure,' he ruled him out of best-seller status. A crucial weakness is a common thing in a detective—for the drink, for the opposite sex, for the same sex, for a little sadism—but the vice will only act as a spice; the real thrust will lie in the capacity this figure has to be a villain, which empowers the capacity to be a saviour. What in Christian theology was the worst heresy, the Manichean view that God had a bad and a good side, is a central mechanism for credibility in a modern world that is both humanist and brutalised.

Extending the genre

Publishers always want something new, but not so new as to frighten book buyers. Sherlock Holmes in a wheelchair might be fine, but as a Martian infiltrator he might have restricted appeal. As a result, much originality in crime fiction is basically a tweaking of previous patterns. Thus Robert B. Parker has an East Coast tough guy who, naturally, went to college. And in the wake of Ellis Peters, we find detectives scattered through most of the scenic periods of English history.

No harm in that: both entertainment and royalties can flow from adding an author's personal expertise to an existing tradition. But the big breakthroughs come from bolder forms of reconstruction, seeing a new shape for the familiar patterns of threat and resolution, usually in radically new settings. That's what Peters herself did, and of course Dashiell Hammett too. But there were still precedents for both patterns—there were tough detectives in the dime novel tradition, and Peters may well have read Lilian de la Torre's remarkable *Sam Johnson: Detector*.

The successful innovation will combine an interesting context and elements of earlier patterns with a real area of underlying anxiety that has not yet been touched, as the private eyes dealt with the new American cities, as feminist thrillers bring gender conflict into the form.

Where might new initiatives be found? As Australia becomes increasingly part of Asia, there is a range of anxiety to be handled through fiction, and writers may do well to look back at the wealth of material from the past about Australians and their mysterious adventures in the islands to the north; in books by Louis Becke and Beatrice Grimshaw, for example. Or even in *Showdown*, by Errol Flynn, a competent journalist who had one decent thriller published before he moved to Hollywood and a larger theatre of activity.

Is it conceivable that unemployment or recession could provide the anxious core of successful crime fiction? The British publisher Pluto largely failed with its series of radical thrillers in the 1980s, not just because the market was either yuppie, feminist, or obsessed with Ellis Peters's Brother Cadfael, but basically because the novels were too overtly political. The best of that kind are in coded form: Julian Rathbone and, with *The Volunteers*, Raymond Williams projected their critique into the near future, just as Poe displaced his stories into France rather than dealing directly with the social strains of his own United States. Imaginative displacements are crucial to the magical workings of crime fiction— and there's a good one at the heart of Conan Doyle's own unemployed-beggar mystery, 'The Man with the Twisted Lip'.

It has been said that it is easier to sell a poorly written novel if it is a crime story, simply because of the demand. That might seem encouraging, in a negative kind of way. But it should also outline the opportunity in the form: there is a vast audience which wants, even needs, to relive these fictions of disorder and harmony restored in just the same way as we need to dream and have fables.

But the writer should remember another compulsory element of the form. The detective always makes some mistakes first; and only succeeds when he or she takes over the investigation as a result of compulsive interest rather than a need to make money. Writers need to do that too, with a tough guy's self-confidence and a clue puzzler's spirit of effortless superiority.

Alan Yates is a model in more than stunning sales and courtesy to interviewers. He saw himself as a folklorist, a storyteller, filling a real need. An honourable craft, he thought it, and one worth enriching with personal commitment. Not ghoulish at all, really.

2 RESEARCH

Sandra Harvey

It was a dark and stormy night . . .

Hell of a cliché, but then January 21, 1991 was one hell of a
night.

I know because I looked it up in the newspaper morgue—
which, for a crime writer, just happens to be one of the richest
(and cheapest) sources for everything from story ideas to those
seemingly trivial tidbits that help make a story seem real.

Truth may be stranger than fiction—and, incredibly, is
often far less credible—but if you want to make your fiction
(or non-fiction) more realistic, then reality is a good place to
start.

If you don't know what you're talking about, so to speak,
before you sit down to write, it's a good bet you'll end up
reading that way.

The answer is research.

Good research doesn't show—but it colours everything.
The reader glides effortlessly through your scenes and in and
around your characters.

Bad research—or no research—sticks out like a thug's leg
in a dark alley. And you can't expect your readers to keep
walking down those kinds of mean streets with you for long.

Where to start

Anywhere and everywhere. If you already have a storyline roughed out in your head, you're a good stride or two in front. If you don't, it shouldn't take you long. Ideas are everywhere, but newspapers are a terrific source: from a one-paragraph brief ('Body Found in Harbour'), to a detailed reconstruction of an actual crime (the Great Bookie Robbery, the nefarious deeds of the Toecutter Gang, the North Shore 'granny killer'), to court reports, to a 'straight' news story such as that about the storms that devastated Sydney's North Shore back on January 21, 1991.

Read the reports of the latter and picture the scene: wealthy homes, trees aplenty; the wind howls for hours on end; the rain thunders down, lightning crashes; power lines are down; phones are out; the police and rescue workers are stretched thin; all is chaos . . . and when it's all over, a young woman is found near her sports car, killed by a single dreadful blow to her head from a huge branch. Such a shame, such a lovely girl. Although there was talk—just talk, mind you—that she was, one doesn't like to speak ill of the dead, but they say she was a, how do you say it, a call girl, yes, a high-class call girl. No doubt with a very interesting list of clients . . .

OK, it's a little corny, but you get the idea: ideas are everywhere. Mix and match bits from the papers with something from a TV show, snatches of a bus stop conversation, your own imagination . . . whatever.

Most libraries keep at least some back copies of a selection of newspapers. The larger libraries keep entire collections on microfiche or database—a great source particularly for historical fiction.

Setting the scene

Imagination is all-important. It is the driving force that carries your readers from A to Z—preferably without wanting to catch too many Zs in between. Even if you're writing non-fiction, it is your imagination that makes your telling of the 'true crime' story different from anyone else's.

But unless you are creating a totally fictitious world, the mundane but necessary details are best drawn from the real world—even if you realistically reconstruct them later in your mind's eye. If you want a character to go wandering down a mean street, well, find yourself a mean street and saunter on down it. (A word of advice: Some mean streets are probably best kept clear of. Your hero may be able to beat off hordes of thugs with one hand tied behind her back, but she's got you looking after her.)

Take notes, make sketches, take photos, take a tape recorder and talk to it as you go along . . . whatever will help you create or re-create the scene realistically for your readers. The effort of actually visiting a place that you want to include in your story—or that you think would be a good model for an imaginary scene—is well worth it. Your writing will almost certainly be more confident; you may well save yourself from embarrassing goofs; your description will ring true; and you'll probably pick up some good ideas just by looking around—a great bit of graffiti, a grotty old building that is 'just right', an old drunk who'd make a good, easily overlooked witness . . .

If you want to describe a particular scene—say, the main drag at Bondi Beach about 10 o'clock on a Saturday night in the middle of winter—visit the place at that time, on that day, in that season, and soak it all up . . . and if there are locals hanging about, don't be shy about striking up a conversation. You never know what they might know. Look around you, listen, smell: what sort of flowers are in bloom? Are there crowds? What sort of people are they? Is it noisy? Is it hot and sticky? Are the garbage bins overflowing? Is it hard to find a parking spot? Anything and everything is worth taking in. You may end up discarding most of it, but you've got to sieve plenty of gravel to find the flecks of gold.

Putting your characters in places that your readers may know works well—when it is done well. If it's not done well, it's a disaster. If the readers start thinking they know more about what you're writing about than you do, don't be surprised, when you look in the rear-view mirror to find that no-one's bothering to follow you any more.

Visiting the scenes of your crimes—preferably not ones against literature—is a must if you are writing non-fiction. Indeed, it's inexcusable not to. You simply cannot rely on newspaper, radio or TV accounts, or even court transcripts—a great source we'll discuss later—to get the flavour of a place. If you can't picture every tiny, precious detail of the scene, your readers won't have a hope. Walk through the park where the murder happened, as close as possible to the time it happened. If the crime occurred in a building, see if you can get access, or at least check it out from outside. If there has been a murder in a house, the chances are good that it will be sold—and therefore be open for inspection. Keep an eye on the real estate section of the local paper for the inspection times and take a look for yourself. True crime writing demands far more disciplined research than crime fiction—for obvious reasons—but it pays off.

> They called it 'Humpshire', and it seemed that almost every other man was round-shouldered from a lifetime hunched over a bench in some tiny workshop. It was here that Chubb and Yale began. The men were so adept at working their metal that they boasted, in their broad accents, that 'Will'null men was born with iron in tha blood'. There have been Glovers in and around Willenhall since 1750, and John Glover, born more than a century later, was by no means the first to turn to keymaking. As soon as he was old enough, he followed his father into the trade.

Sounds simple enough, and so it should, but it took six weeks and a trip halfway around the world. The passage, from *The Killer Next Door*, was drawn from bags full of information gathered during a research trip to Britain—bits and pieces found in the Wolverhampton public library, newspaper archives, and interviews with the members of 'granny killer' John Glover's family and with friends and neighbours who remembered them from 50 years ago. It didn't help that the family was so itinerant, nor that the one place that they had ever called home had long ago been razed.

True crime or fiction, always keep an eye out that whatever you are writing makes sense and is consistent—that it rings true. It may seem an all-too-obvious warning, but there are more than enough published stories out there that missed this point to make it worth stressing again and again.

Now, realism is all very well if it's just a matter of a cab ride and a stroll around. But what if your story is set in, say, New Orleans—and you don't happen to have the air fare this week? It's tough, but you're tougher. Or at least more resourceful. If you can't experience it first hand, you'll have to rely on secondary sources. Think of them as eye witnesses that you've got to dig up, then squeeze information out of. Use your imagination and nous to track down the types of secondary sources most suited to what you want to describe, but any of the following would be a good bet for getting a feel for out-of-the-way places:

- *Libraries*: They are always excellent places to dig up information. By all means explain to the librarians what you are after. Information is the name of their game: if they don't have it, they may well have some good ideas about where to go. You would probably be best looking for: street maps of the particular town, photos, books, magazines, newspapers, videos. Similarly, if any or all of your story is set in the past, the library is a great place to dig out good details. Newspapers can provide information on mundane things like the cost of living and the news of the day; other helpful sources are historical records, books, and accounts of specific incidents.
- *Travel agencies or tourist offices*: At the least they might have brochures about the town or area you are interested in. Again, if you explain what you are after, they may be able to give you advice on where else to go.
- *People*: They are always the best sources, because they're 'interactive'. Talking to them can turn up all sorts of facts no-one would think of putting in a book otherwise.

The same principle applies to just about any other scenes or experiences you might want to render realistically. A board meeting of a big company? I've never been to one, either, but plenty of people have—and have written about it. Try non-fiction books on corporate takeovers, or the public relations officers at any of the big companies. Likewise for anything from life on a sheep station, to insider trading, to political high- and low-life, to the inside dope on life in a convent. There are books aplenty that tell all on just about any situation you can 'imagine'.

The body on page two

The crime is the pivotal point of your story. More often than not, the crime is murder. Get the details right, but don't overdo it. A lack of gore doesn't mean a lack of suspense or horror—in fact, the reverse is more likely. But although less is better—in the telling—you should aim to *know* as much as you can: the more you know, the better you can write less.

Most crime books involve the crime: murder. But the reality is few people have even seen a real 'live' dead body, let alone a murdered one. This can make it tough to get it right, but, as ever, there are plenty of eyewitnesses and experts to help you out. Try any of the following, for starters:

- *Morgues*: Obviously, they are full of dead bodies. But more importantly, they are staffed by people who know much much more than you'll ever need to—or probably want to—about corpses . . . and murder. In particular, most morgues employ or are associated with forensic pathologists, whose job it is to know what happens to bodies during and after they are stabbed, shot, strangled or otherwise messed about with. Morgue staff can also help you with the mundane but necessary details about how a murder is officially handled: what happens at the crime scene; how the body is transported; and, of course, the crucial post-mortem examination, or autopsy.

   If your local morgue doesn't run to a public relations officer, try the coroner's office direct. The City Morgue, at Glebe, in Sydney, which handles about 2600 corpses a year, has open days and guided tours about twice a year. As well as the official morgues, many large hospitals have their own morgues. And most major universities have departments within their medical faculties which undertake forensic research and perform dissections. These may also be well worth contacting, even if they only direct you to some relevant reading material. They usually have open days too at some stage during the year.

- *Court records*: Frustratingly—especially if you are doing research on an actual crime—court records are not necessarily as easy to get hold of as would appear from the movies, but they can be great sources of detail about death. If a coronial inquiry was held—and in NSW, at least, this is mandatory in all cases in which a death is suspicious or unusual—then the Coroner's Office will have tucked away somewhere a nice thick file of documents ranging from courtroom transcript to detailed post-mortem results to police reports. The documents will almost certainly be choked with jargon, but there will be some gems among it all. Try this:

> On the posterior surface of the scalp, in the region of the occiput, was a T-shaped laceration, straddling the midline and 144cm above the level of the heel. The transverse component of the laceration was 3.8cm in length . . .

The woman in question had a cut on her head, in other words. And that—taken from a pathologist's post-mortem examination report—is a comparatively lucid example. But struggle through it. It's important that you digest this kind of detail so you can pass on to your readers something much easier to swallow but still true to life—or death.

If someone has been charged with the murder, the matter moves on to the criminal courts proper, and the file grows accordingly. The bulk of it will be taken up with what is called the police 'brief' (for brief of evidence—although there is rarely anything brief about it). This can be a treasure trove. It will contain pretty much everything you would need to know about the crime, from an evidentiary point of view anyway. Key information will include:

a. Clinical but thorough descriptions of the crime scene, recording everything from the position of the body and probable cause of death to what the corpse was wearing and what, if anything, of interest was found nearby.

b. Statements from every man and his dog: the person who discovered the body; ambulance officers who examined it; the uniformed police who reached the scene first; witnesses, if any; neighbours; investigating detectives; doctors who pronounced that the victim was dead; forensic pathologists who conducted the post-mortem; the relative who identified the body; friends; lovers; husbands; wives . . . anyone and everyone who the investigators believe have something worth saying about the deceased or the death.

As with post-mortem reports, you may have to struggle through some jargon, but there are many rich seams of information just below the unattractive surface. Here, for example, is a homicide squad detective's statement:

> I entered the house and on a landing near the kitchen door I saw the body of a female person . . . Without disturbing the scene, a search was made to locate vital signs, however none were found and it was believed that she was dead. With the aid of a torch I proceeded to search the house . . .

Zero marks for captivating prose, but then that's *your* job. Which in the above case would not be too hard: the house was in pitch darkness, the cop had left his gun at home . . . and there was a killer waiting somewhere inside.

Even seemingly trivial detail in a witness's statement can be put to good effect. This is from a 10-year-old boy:

> Matthew and I decided to go outside and see if we could find the bus and get my boater back . . . We went to the security entrance area on the ground floor of the units where I saw an old lady lying face down . . .

Not only were the two boys the first ones to discover the body, and therefore crucial witnesses, but notice how they came to find it: the boy had left his school hat on the bus. A seemingly trivial detail but a lovely way to lead the reader to the murder scene.

Police briefs are marvellous—perhaps indispensable—sources not only for true-crime writers but also for those who simply want to give their stories a realistic feel. However, getting hold of them is not always easy and will be nearly impossible if the case has not yet been closed, even though, theoretically, they become public documents once tendered in court. To get access, try the public relations offices of both the police service and the court administration.

The *court transcript* is a record of everything that was said in court, even while the jury was not present. The transcript may or may not include various documents that were tendered to the court as evidence: psychiatric reports, incidental statements and the like. Getting hold of transcript is not always easy—and certainly not cheap—though its availability varies depending largely on the particular jurisdiction. Your first contact would be the Clerk of the Court. Explain what you want and ask for his advice.

On the trail

The hunt—or the solving of the case—forms the basis of most crime stories whether they are fictional or true-crime: the pieces of the puzzle slowly come together, and the crescendo of suspense builds to an exciting climax. But no matter how good the end, it never justifies shoddy means. Getting your readers to that thrilling finish depends largely on getting them to believe every twist and turn you've put in the path that leads them there. Investigations follow logical paths. Sure, there are lucky breaks and setbacks, and there are plenty of different roads a man can walk down to get where he's got to go—just make sure that whichever one you choose covers some realistic terrain along the way.

Most investigators—from police to private eyes to humble insurance assessors—will tell you that most of what they do is plain boring. While that may be true, there's no reason why your *writing* has to imitate reality quite so closely. On the other hand, nor is there any reason to ignore the reality of the routine of an investigation. One of the appealing things about

Sue Grafton's Kinsey Millhone, for instance, is that she *does* the dull, ordinary, everyday stuff—and, far from it being boring or detracting from the storyline, it adds to the realism. The actual process of an investigation not only can be interesting of itself, but should be a device for luring the reader deeper and deeper into the story.

So how does an investigator investigate? The first thing to remember is the truism that the first 24 hours of a murder inquiry are the most crucial. If the investigators have not got a strong lead or suspect by the end of that period, they are in for a long, hard slog—which, of course, may well be exactly what you want to put your hero through. To track down details on the standard operating procedure for an investigation, the best place to start, not surprisingly, is the police. It is unlikely that you will be able to get access to the official police rules and regulations that set out (in tedious technical detail) how to begin, conduct and wind up an investigation, but you may well be able to dig out something similar from a library. At any rate, contact the police public relations office and see how you go. Although police tend to be overly wary about any inquiries they think may be critical, they can be surprisingly open and helpful.

Two recent ABC-TV drama series, *Phoenix* and *Janus*, owe much of their realistic feel to months of research undertaken with the cooperation of the Victorian police. Researchers for the shows were given enviable access to police 'in the field', enabling them to, in effect, live with the cops for weeks at a time to get a feel for how they really operate.

Former police are also a great source of information about the nitty-gritty of police work, and they are usually far more talkative than those still in the job. To make contact, try the local police union or retired officers' association. Or try any of the hundreds of private investigators in the phone book. Many of them are former police, and even those who are not can give you a rundown on the basics of investigative techniques.

A more intensive but potentially very rewarding way of finding out how police do their work is to enlist as a volunteer. The community-based scheme, which operates in most

Australian states, involves training people to assist police, mainly administratively. In NSW, the course includes several weekends at the Police Academy learning the basics of police operations, then working with uniformed police at local stations.

No matter what type of crime or activity your story demands, there is someone out there who is an expert on it and can tell you enough to make your version sound real. Your hero has to pick a lock? Visit your local locksmith and ask what is involved. You can be sure it'll take more than magically running a credit card up and down the door jamb. Need a run-down on alarms and sensor pads? Try the phone book for vendors of security systems. Want a spot of arson to add some flair to your story? Try the fire brigade or insurance assessors. They'll be able to tell you not only how to light a good blaze but also how a good investigator can pick through the smouldering rubble and ashes and work out what happened. What sort of hole does a .22 rifle make when fired into a body at close range? Try anyone from manufacturers to shooters' magazines (the type you get in newsagents, not gun stores) to forensic pathologists to your friendly local librarian. If your hero's car has to have an accident, you might be wondering what would be the best way for the bad guys to tamper with it. Any grease monkey should be able to set you straight on that.

No matter what you can come up with, someone out there knows how it's done.

The goodies, the baddies and the unlikely

Creating and developing your characters—heroes, villains, and everyone in between—is one of the most challenging and potentially rewarding aspects of writing. The reward is in bringing a character to life; the challenge, obviously, is in fashioning that credible persona—and ensuring that what he or she does is believable.

- Make sure your characters have reasons for doing whatever they do (even mindless violence needs a motive): don't let your hero jump back in her car if she's just going next door.

- Make sure that if your characters start doing something they keep on doing it: it will be not only bizarre but infuriating if your hero's red Porsche suddenly and inexplicably becomes a black BMW. Red herrings are all very well but if something, or some activity, was worth mentioning in the first place, then your readers are well within their rights to assume it's relevant.

- Make sure your characters don't do the impossible: no matter how snazzy your hero's car may be, it is going to take her longer than ten minutes to drive from the centre of Sydney to Palm Beach.

If you are writing fiction, you pretty much have *carte blanche* with your characters. If your bent is true crime, you are stuck with what the good Lord gave you—which can sometimes be pretty ordinary. Clearly, one of the best ways to find out about real characters is to sit down and talk with them, watch them at work, play or whatever activity is relevant, and then try your best to present a realistic picture of the person.

There are differing views about how much licence you are allowed in true crime. I think the best policy is to be as honest as possible. Some tips:

- No matter how big your ego, you can *never* get inside someone else's head. Not even a psychiatrist who had been treating someone for most of their life could honestly claim to have achieved this, so don't pretend you have, even if you did manage to get to know the person you are writing about.
- Don't put conversations in quotation marks unless you are *certain* those words were said. If someone tells you that particular words were said, fair enough. Similarly if the words have been recorded in a statement or court transcript. Quotation marks are meant to indicate that those precise words were spoken—and not that words something like them were said, or might have been said, or even should have been said. There is nothing wrong, or less

dramatic, with paraphrasing—or even constructing conversation without using quotation marks:

> Bullshit! he yelled. I never said any such thing.
> Did so, she replied—a little too sheepishly.

- Following on from both of the above: do not put thoughts into a character's head unless you *know* this is what they thought. To do otherwise is facile and dishonest.

Court in the act

Most crime stories—even true-crime books—climax with the case being solved, which usually entails the baddie being caught and led off in cuffs by the constabulary. They generally omit the tedious details of court hearings and trials, and the possibility that the bad guy may well get off in the end. But even if the judicial process seems like too much of a long and drawn-out anti-climax to include in your story, it would be well worth your while spending a day or two sitting in on a criminal trial. Not only are they a good source of information, they can be fascinating—as the O.J. Simpson case has proved in the US. In Australia, the Megan Kalazjich murder trial captivated Scobie Malone's creator, Jon Cleary. He sat in on the first day's hearing, intending just to get a taste, and stayed on for the entire 12 weeks of the trial. Cleary says the experience was invaluable, and he has drawn on it several times in subsequent stories.

Be warned: tedious legal argument can send even the most seasoned court watcher to sleep. On the whole, though, the courts—from local to district and on up to the supreme courts—can provide you with all the colour you need to form the basis of a good story: a parade of cops and crims, barristers and solicitors, expert witnesses and ordinary people, unbelievable alibis and amazing tales. Check the daily newspapers for what's on and where. Most courts are open to the public, although there are certain rules and etiquette, particularly about taking notes (a no-no without permission). Check with the Clerk of the Court's Office or the reception desk at the courts for what you can and can't do.

Another worthwhile outing is the Justice and Police Museum in Sydney; other cities may offer something similar. Although much of the material and exhibits are historical, the museum boasts an impressive selection of confiscated weapons, from knuckledusters to flick knives.

Research can be boring, or it can be fun. Enjoy the adventure.

3 FACT INTO FICTION

Kerry Greenwood

Where do ideas come from?

'Where do you get your ideas from?' you cry. And I answer, 'Haven't the faintest idea.' 'I just take my bucket to the well of stories and see what sort of fish swim to the surface.' 'I dream them.'

I am lying.

Only because the explanation takes so long. Ideas come from everywhere. Everything that has ever happened to you, gentle reader, everything you have ever heard, read, seen, watched or suffered is material. When you write, you are mining your own mind, dipping your quill in your own heart and writing with your blood. Writers are vultures, eavesdroppers, exploiters of other people's pains and pleasures. We steal our characters and situations from life as brazenly and automatically as a crow picks out a lamb's eyes. And we use ourselves just as shamelessly.

That is why writing fiction is sometimes as exhausting and difficult as walking a tightrope across the Grand Canyon with a cast iron stove strapped to one leg.

Researching the real world

The thing about doing research is that you should end up knowing five times as much as you can ever use. This is essential to avoid either 1) the failing, common in historical fiction, of 'putting it all in'—'See how much I know about 1928!'—and boring the reader catatonic, or 2) not knowing enough about your subject and dropping into anachronism, which is very easy, and thus proving yourself untrustworthy. This can ruin the book for some readers. You will get letters, stinkers that begin, 'Dear Madam, Are you aware that the Ballarat train has never had a dining car?' It sometimes seems a pity to me that I know, or knew for as long as it took me to write a given book, such a lot about a particular subject which I have not been able to use in the book and won't use again. But the important thing is that I know it while I'm writing. That way, the details just slot into conversations and descriptions. I can't write a whole novel set in a grey, plasticine landscape. I have to know what, for instance, Phryne would see if she stood at the corner of Heffernan Lane on a cold night in 1928. Otherwise I can't write the book.

Research is therefore essential, but the knowledge that results must be carried lightly. Begin always with newspapers. Most state libraries keep complete sets but you may have to order them from storage; ring up and ask. Your local library can be looted for all its books on a subject (heaven help the poor kid who was doing a major assignment on ancient Greece when I was writing *Cassandra*). If you don't have an idea, then browse. Have a wander through the archives and see what pops up. Look at a real case, a real crime, and follow it up. University law libraries keep law reports and librarians will show you how to understand case citation if you ask them nicely. Reports of trials are always fascinating. (But criminal case reports only began in the 1960s; before that you have to either look at Appeals to the Supreme Court, which include the facts of the case and original trial, or read the newspapers. *Truth* always has the sensational details.) Read a cross-section of the papers, from the radical to the conservative and don't forget the local suburban paper. You can also obtain coroners reports, ring the Coroner's office, and go and watch some inquests. Don't get too narrowly focused. The case next to the one you are supposed to be reading might be more fascinating. If you know any police, talk to them and don't be too shocked by their black humour, which they share with doctors, nurses, morgue attendants and duty solicitors. If you want to know how the court system works, go to a magistrates court, especially the central court in any capital city after a public holiday, and sit there all day. Look at faces. Listen to the voices, the words used, the slang. Look, for instance, at how a person's posture alters when they are in handcuffs, and look at the escorting officer. He stands differently, too. If you can coopt a lawyer, go into the cells and watch the prisoners. Note everything—especially the smells.

You can get basic police procedure from the *Police Standing Orders*, which are availabe from government bookshops. The ABC-TV series *Janus* was very accurate. If you want to approach a police officer for advice, try ringing the police archives in your city and asking them to recommend an approach. Do not walk into a local station on a busy morning and ask the overworked desk sergeant a lot of vague questions.

Nothing can replace actually walking your setting. Once, in Hamilton, I was walking along Grey Street, where a circus was going to go for the finale of *Blood and Circuses*. I had a map and directory entries and the memories of several old people, and the street had not changed much structurally since 1928. Suddenly, overlaid on the new buildings and day-glo signs, I could see the old street, sepia, like an old photograph. The vision lasted long enough for me to stop dead and be run into by a passing pram, and once we had untangled ourselves and apologised, it was gone. But for one moment I saw Hamilton as it was in 1928. I don't know if this was vision or creative visualisation, but it was wonderful and it gave me a really good description of the street. Put on your hiking boots and hit the toe. If you are a concrete-details writer like me, you need to know not only what your setting looks like, but what it feels like and smells like.

I suggest you play the train game. On a long journey, imagine yourself on a desert island with the other people currently occupying your carriage. How would they react to each other (and to you)? Which one—or ones—would you choose as a lover and how would they all react to, say, the murder of one of their number? How would that young man who has obviously been crossed in love relate to the girl with green hair and chains? Would the stout man in overalls reveal unexpected leadership skills? Would the knitting ladies cope with the tropical sun—and why are they so pale, anyway? I beguiled the tedious journey from Footscray to Springvale for a whole term with this game and it never palled. It's an exercise—if you need an excuse—in character creation.

Writing a crime story is fun. It allows you to kill people you don't like in various gruesome ways. If you wish for exact advice on, say, dosages of poison, then consult a textbook, such as dear old *Glaister on Poisons*. Ferret around a second-hand bookshop or three for texts, and also for memoirs of forensic pathologists, which are always good for a few ideas. I recommend the *Notable British Trials* series, which is as good as reading the actual case records. Colin Wilson is my favourite theorist on the reasons why people commit crimes. The *Encyclopaedia of Murder* and the *Encyclopaedia of Modern Murder* are also very helpful.

If you are basing your victim or murderer closely on a real person, be careful. Christina Stead was the world's most hated house guest for her habit of taking her dear friends and putting them in books, terribly recognisable, as villains. This can only lead to a lonely old age drinking martinis for breakfast. Most people will not recognise themselves anyway, but if they have any unusual attributes—i.e., if you were using me, red hair, duty solicitor, writer of crime novels, living with a wizard—it would be unsafe to include them. If you feel you need to use the facts, cut them out in the final draft.

Look at people on a tram or bus and listen to their conversations; remember, writers are vultures. When I was travelling on the women writers' train in 1991, we were at dinner somewhere and a really riveting domestic argument was going on at the next table. I was about to politely stop listening when I realised that every woman at that table—poet, novelist and social historian alike—had put her mouth onto automatic pilot and was listening. You might have thought eavesdropping was your private vice; I did, but it isn't. Other people are endlessly fascinating. And they are all material.

Fictionalising your own experience

Writing can bleach the pain out of a personal experience, too, but only when the reality has been safely distanced. Writing that comes out of raw pain and personal conviction is bad writing. I was in Greece once when a climber fell off Parnassus and died in my arms. I sat like the Pietà (noting that the Madonna's way is the only way to hold a dying man) while a sixteen-year-old boy called me his mother, vomited arterial blood all over my white shirt so that it was glued to my skin, and died. His ribs were all broken and he felt wrong under my hands. I was rescued by the local bus driver, Spiro, who took us all back to Delphi and we sat up all night praying and drinking Metaxa and weeping, which mitigated my shock. But I was shattered. The scene kept on replaying itself in front of my eyes. I scrubbed my skin raw and still smelt blood. I had skinned my feet scrambling up the rocks and I had stone dust in my hair. I didn't know what to do with the shirt—I couldn't wash it and I didn't feel that I could throw it away—so I took it back to the sacred site and buried it. A passing old man who might have been Pan himself told me, 'The gods require sacrifices.' Add to this that it was Maundy Thursday, which the Greeks call 'Bloody Thursday', and that it happened at Delphi, an awesomely mythic place, and you can imagine my state.

So I began to write about it. I wrote an account for the Greek cops. I wrote it again with all the details—the smell of blood, the shattering noise of the falling stone, the weight of the young man as he died. Then I changed the narrative voice from 'me' to 'she' and wrote it again. By the time I got to Tuscany the pain had almost gone and I had the first chapter of *Death at Victoria Dock*. The accident happened to Phryne, not me, on page 2. And she coped with it much better.

> She pulled off her coat, lest it be stained, and slid a silk-clad arm under the figure, whom she could now see was a very

young man with a shock of uncut tow-coloured hair, muddied from the road. His head lolled on her shoulder; under her exploring hands his body felt broken. There was massive damage to his ribs. They were spongy under her fingers, and a hole in his neck the size of a crown piece was pumping blood . . . It was a high-boned, Slavic face. The chin had never been shaved. He was paling to tallow. His whole body was slackening into death. He drew a dreadful blood-filled breath and said quite clearly 'Ma mére est à Riga,' retched, and died.

Phryne held him close as blood fountained from his lungs and flooded her shirt. Then she freed a hand, closed his eyes, and gently laid him down. A foolish courtesy, she thought as she lowered his head, cradled in her hand, for no roughness could hurt him now. He looked heart-breakingly young—no more than seventeen.

Later, Phryne also gets to do what I longed to do and could not—tear off the bloody shirt. She is a classic wish-fulfilment figure.

Ruddy Gore: How fact became fiction

My book *Ruddy Gore* started from a desire to do a murder on stage, because Ngaio Marsh, Agatha Christie and other Golden Age writers did this often. They usually chose plays like *Hamlet* or *Macbeth*, where there is a fair chance of being spiked by a prop. As I am also a parodist and a G and S fan, I decided to use a Gilbert and Sullivan opera. This book was a present for my sister Janet, so I asked her what she would like. My sister wanted a ghost, and the only ghost in G and S is in *Ruddigore*, which also gave me the title for the book—*Ruddy Gore*. I knew that I had to use Her Majesty's because that was the only theatre that did G and S in Melbourne at the time. The Maj., as Melburnians call it, is on the corner of Little Bourke Street—Melbourne's Chinatown—so that gave me a Chinese subplot.

So I sent out my invaluable mother, who is my tireless researcher, and gave her a list of questions. I needed to know:

If *Ruddigore* was performed in 1928.

All she could find out about the production: pictures, reviews, etc.

Who owned the businesses in Little Bourke Street: map, directory.

The history of the street.

General history of *Ruddigore*, production details etc.

My researcher went to the state library and consulted the 1928 city directory, which listed who lived at each house and their profession. From this she copied the pages relating to Little Bourke Street. She then walked along the street, checking what had changed. She went to the Chinese Museum and bought me a Cantonese phrase book (having ascertained that Cantonese was spoken by the traders), and she talked to the museum staff (who were very helpful). She made copious notes.

Then I went to the local library, borrowed an armload of general history books on Melbourne, and leafed through them, looking for pictures. The plot was still inchoate but I had a photograph of a Chinese hawker and a fruit seller. I also had the memoranda and articles of the See Yup Society, about which I was curious.

The Performing Arts Museum has a scrapbook relating to G and S productions in Melbourne. It told us that *Ruddigore* was only performed once in 1928, for the arrival of the pioneer aviator Bert Hinkler. Note that if you are on the right track, coincidences start working for you. They call it synchronicity, or the Library Angel. Not having been put on for years, *Ruddigore* is being performed by the Australian Opera in 1995. The scrapbook gave me several newspaper accounts of the Hinkler Gala, which Phryne would naturally go to, being a flyer. The book, I decided, would begin with her arriving at the theatre.

I didn't yet know anything else about it. I talked to a Cantonese-speaking friend about the Chinese in Australia and walked Little Bourke Street myself. I consulted books and watched the Chinese Museum's film *The Second Gold Mountain*. I sent my indefatigable researcher to the Police Archives to see what she could find about crime in 1928 involving the Chinese (and, if possible, the rules of fan tan). I read two books on Hinkler and refreshed my memory about his plane, noticing that of all the flyers Hinkler was the only one who didn't give his aircraft a name. I filed away this fact for future reference. (It turned out not to be significant.)

I found the perfect cloak for Phryne in a 1928 issue of *Vogue*. I decided that she would wear a Mercury costume and sketched it. I re-read *The Outlaws of the Marsh*, deciding to take my names from it. I also re-read the *Tao Teh Ching* for details of Taoism, and a book on Sun Yat Sen and the Chinese revolution. I decided to call Phryne's lover Lin Chung. I knew what he looked like because I had seen 'him' in a photograph of a young man in the Star Ballroom in Shanghai in a biography of Noel Coward, who wrote a play in that city. I called on my own memories of Shanghai, the bamboo washing poles above the street, the crowded houses, the Bund and the Yangtse Kiang, and the sound of Cantonese, which is clear, staccato and more guttural than Mandarin. I recalled walking into a tea house in rural China—a 154cm, fat, redheaded blue-eyed foreign devil—and the courtesy with which the people avoided staring at me. I asked a police prosecutor who used to be in the Victorian gaming squad about fan tan. I listened to the voice of an old Chinese woman talking about the revolution and heard the way she stressed the wrong syllables, though her voice was perfectly modulated, her accent Eton-and-Oxford and her English better than mine. I considered what social imperatives Phryne was outraging by taking a Chinese lover, read the newspapers of the time, and looked into contemporary theories of eugenics and racial superiority. (Disgust never stopped me from researching—one cannot allow oneself the luxury of not reading something because it's abhorrent.) I mined everyone's memory for information on the Chinese and G and S operettas. I read three biographies of J.S. Gilbert and one of Sullivan and stripped my local library of its G and S books. I visited Jan Gordon Clark, whose grandmother was a costume mistress for The Maj. I examined her sewing machine and mended a silk dress while she told me all about her grandmother and showed me photos and memorabilia.

I drew on my own stage experience. I talked to Matthew Gordon Clark, a lighting technician, about lighting and about how technicians feel about actors. I had been a stage manager for several plays at school, and I recalled how I had felt about actors. I got as much technical information as I could and then asked The Maj. if I could have a guided tour. I walked the whole theatre, recalling that it was rebuilt in 1929 after being destroyed by fire. The managers gave me a photocopy of a brief history and my remarkable and gifted researcher found me a photo of the old theatre. My assumption that the layout was more or less the same as that of the new one was confirmed when Jan Gordon Clark sent me a floor plan. I noted how the theatre smelt and what it felt like, and offended the management by telling them that I was giving them a ghost—the Princess has a ghost, but not The Maj. I asked my mother to tell me everything she could remember about my great uncle Gwilym, who was a G and S singer, and decided to put him in the novel as an exceptionally charming bounder. Every family has stories. Go and talk to your family.

Then I researched the Spiritualist church, since I'd decided a medium was going to be needed, and read several tomes on stage magic and a life of Ching Lin Soo, the most famous Chinese magician, whom I had heard of through Ray Bradbury's novel *Something Wicked This Way Comes*. I read several 1920s reports by the Society for Psychical Research (supported by Sir Arthur Conan Doyle, by the way) and a few weird books by mediums of the time. I also looked at the Fraudulent Mediums Act and records of prosecutions under it in the Supreme Court library.

Then I taped *Ruddigore* from my grandfather's G and S collection and listened to the whole opera three times. By then I knew how it was produced, what everyone was wearing, how they sounded, how they moved, how the lighting and sets were produced and made. I knew a lot about G and S generally and about the original production of *Ruddigore* as well. I knew exactly who lived where in Little Bourke Street in 1928. I guessed that you would be able to smell the bananas in the warehouse which now houses the Chinese Museum because I could smell the museum's incense in the Maj. basement. I knew what Phryne was wearing, where she was going and with whom, and what she would hear.

Then I waited. I cannot force a book. It organises itself; I can't push it. A week after I had sort of finished the research—one never really finishes research—I woke at 3 a.m. from a vivid dream of Phryne leaping into a fight in the cold darkness of the cobbled street and knew I had a novel coming on.

Then I wrote day and night for three weeks. I had a G and S–style plot, so I had lost children, birthmarks, and ghosts—I wanted to reflect the plot of *Ruddigore* in the novel. And I was delighted when Lin Chung arrived in the first chapter and turned out to be a stage magician, one of the strong men of the Temple of the War God whom I had seen performing in Beijing. My Chinese friend Foong Ling Kong helped me with Cantonese dialect, read the Chinese bits, and approved them as 'very Chinese'. They included my walk down Little Bourke Street, the politeness I'd experienced in that Chinese cafe in 1985, and my own experience of love-making which does not depend on penetration—though I am not going to disclose the name of my research assistant in that matter. The theatre parts were read by Matthew the tech, who corrected the bits I had got wrong, and Jan, who approved of my general theatrical ambiance and the portrait of her grandmother. My researcher read the whole manuscript and approved of it. My friend Jenny Pausacker also read it, and suggested some adjustments in the plot.

Then it was finished and Kathy Hope, my editor at McPhee–Gribble, who is a Phryne fan, picked up the discrepancies and corrected the abominable punctuation. I hate punctuation. It interrupts my flow.

How much of this book was me and how much assembled historical detail? About half and half. I use my experience and my life, and everything I can find out about the period and setting.

I do not know how I construct plots, because I don't construct them. They arise from the strange, organic, possessed way that I write. The most useful thing I can tell a new writer is not to listen to advice. Read a lot of detective stories, by everyone from Edgar Allan Poe to Ruth Rendell, and analyse how they get their effects. Then work out how you, yourself, personally, write, which is as individual as the way that you, yourself, personally make love. A very neat person may need to know exactly what is going to happen in each chapter. If I do that I am too bored to write the novel. John Buchan observed that it is easy to plant clues and make a reasonable story out of three seemingly unconnected facts because the author is working backwards. I always work forwards and let the clues fall where they may, and they are always in the right place. There is no rule save that there are no rules. A novel is not a set of short stories tied together. It has its own weight, balance and impetus. Everyone has their own way of writing it and if it works, then it's right.

Writers are vultures, the sacred vultures of Isis, perhaps, who transmuted base flesh into divine spirit. The world is your meat. Go out there and observe, watch, listen, store, digest it. Read widely and omnivorously, talk to as many people as you can, pay attention to the world. But in the end, up against the wall, it is only you.

EXERCISES

1. Recall an incident in your life when you felt a vivid surge of emotion (fear is a good one for a crime story) and write about it. Describe the circumstances, describe the sensation of the emotion. What did it feel like, what did you see, hear, smell, touch?

2. Now, take the authenticity of that emotion and give it to your fictional character. Use your imagination to create fictional circumstances in which your character can feel that emotion, e.g. a bank hold-up, a gun in the back in a quiet suburban street.

4 PLOT AND STRUCTURE

Garry Disher

PLOT

How often have we said of a crime novel: 'It tells a good yarn but the characters are wooden' or 'I like the characters but the story is predictable'? Plot and character are the central elements of crime fiction—indeed, of all traditional fiction—and this chapter argues that they are inextricably linked. The best and most satisfying stories and novels tell a good story *and* involve us in the lives of the characters. Plot is not a fixed edifice upon which characters may be hung like cups on cupboard hooks; nor should plot be overshadowed by an overindulgence in character, or forced in unlikely directions by characters behaving illogically. The best crime writers aim to achieve a fine balance between plot-direction and character-direction in their work.

Starting points

There can be no plot until there is a crime. Experienced crime writers commonly have more ideas for crimes, criminal characters, heroes, scenes and incidents than they could hope to explore in a lifetime of writing. They draw on personal experiences (for example, being burgled), the experiences of others (an acquaintance's conviction for fraud), conventional plot situations from films and novels (a private eye taking on a missing person's case), speculation (asking: What if . . . ? My short story 'Threshold' grew out of the question: 'What if one of the policemen investigating a murder were in fact the murderer?'), interesting characters (Peter Corris based Cliff Hardy in part on his uncles), actual crimes (my story 'Trusthouse' was suggested by the disappearance of the Beaumont children), news stories (my files are bulging with newspaper clippings about crimes, trials, criminal psychology and police investigations), contemporary issues (Sara Paretsky's novels explore pollution scandals, political corruption and social justice debates), witnessed incidents (a bitter argument in a cafe), endings (all I knew before I wrote the story 'Old Ground' was that the body of a missing man would be discovered concealed under a buried coffin) and beginnings (Sean O'Faolain's classic brew: a character, a situation and a promise).

But what of the crime at the centre of the story? We tend automatically to think 'murder' (and it could be argued that there must always be a murder at some point in crime fiction), but murder may simply be the fallout from another, more compelling crime or mystery. The real issue at the heart of Ruth Rendell's *Kissing the Gunner's Daughter* is not the horrifying massacre of a family but an inner corruption at work in that family which leads to the massacre. Other crimes might be embezzlement, blackmail, bribery, industrial espionage, kidnap and theft. Certainly the central crime must be significant—for the characters involved and in terms of relative weight—but crime novels no longer devote themselves solely to puzzles, with police or amateur detectives solving unlikely and uninvolving murders in locked rooms in English manor houses on stormy weekends. A good crime novel will work on three main levels: as a mystery or adventure, as a critique of society, and as an account of character. A murder involves emotions, after all; it has a context, and deserves serious treatment.

Before we can see the potential of the material in our files, however, we must be able to imagine committing a crime or at least imagine our way into the minds of characters who could. The ability to acknowledge a darker side of the self is an essential attribute in a crime writer. If we have never fantasised about a foolproof way of robbing a bank or of harming someone who has done us wrong, if we have never been curious about a crime reported by the media or recognised its imaginative possibilities, then we should not be writing crime fiction.

Character and plot

Whether or not you have a villain in mind first, or a particular crime, characters determine the way we enter, tell and shape a story. Character is action, and actions grow out of character. The English novelist John Galsworthy said that character is plot. The unfolding of a plot is dependent upon fictional characters making particular decisions in response to problems they have to solve, and the kinds of decisions they make are governed by their personalities. It is our job to know our fictional characters well. If personality and motivation are thoroughly understood, then plotting becomes easier, and characters will be more alive and believable on the page.

In crime fiction we tend to meet characters of extraordinary ability: they can shoot a gun, disarm a knife-wielding killer, recognise anomalies at a murder scene, break into a bank vault, question a devious suspect, gain access to computer records, escape from a jail, install a wiretap, avoid being tailed. By the nature of their roles, characters in crime fiction also tend to have the kinds of face-to-face confrontations that would leave most of us tense and fearful: betrayal by another gang member, demotion by someone in authority, arrest and imprisonment, calming a psychopath, challenging the rich and powerful with evidence that proves their guilt. Actions like these are also likely to be important incidents in the plot, arising out of earlier actions and leading to later ones.

And so we must ask ourselves, as we plan and as we write: What's motivating him? Where did she learn how to do that? How would he react at this point? What will result if he does X instead of Y?

And so the plot begins to take shape.

Point of view

Point of view—sometimes called voice—influences the way readers gain their information and governs the perspective they have on events, characters and themes. It must be taken into account when plotting a story or novel because it involves deciding which character (or characters) will convey the story, how much they know, how the story will be told, and the tone or 'personality' of the work.

The two most commonly used points of view are:

third person (limited): 'Wyatt knew that Rossiter wanted to chat. Rossiter wanted to chat because he was nervy, but also because it was what people did. Wyatt never felt nervy and he never made small talk out of habit, but he was prepared to make an effort when he wanted information from somebody, like now.'

first person: 'I disliked him on sight. He had the born-to-rule arrogance and well-fed complacency of a private school bully and I was going to enjoy wiping the smirk off his face.'

Third person limited or intimate, so-called because it concentrates wholly on one character's viewpoint, is one of the most widely used and popular voices in fiction. It is less immediate and intimate than first person, in which the narrator is actually a character in the story. First person is the favoured point of view in private eye stories and novels. Both are suspenseful because readers are just as much in the dark as the hero they have come to know, like and trust.

There are certain weaknesses and limitations in both points of view. Readers cannot know what other characters are thinking, or doing off stage, except through what the main character infers or later learns. Also, writers filtering the story through a single character's consciousness must always consider the ways in which factors such as age, class, sex, nationality, education and personality colour that character's perceptions.

Many writers choose the third-person multiple viewpoint, in which alternating chapters or passages reveal the thoughts and actions of each of the main players. A possible weakness is that tension and suspense can be weakened if readers learn too much; on the other hand, readers may feel a heightened tension as they watch the villain manoeuvring behind the scenes against the unsuspecting hero. Another potential weakness is lack of focus, especially if used in a short story, and especially if all the characters and actions are given equal weight.

Less common in contemporary novels is the omniscient point of view, which reads as a general statement not linked to a character's thoughts or perceptions, e.g. 'It is a truth universally acknowledged that a single man in possession of a good fortune must be in want of a wife.' (Jane Austen, *Pride and Prejudice*).

Choosing the appropriate point of view is usually not a problem. Often it simply feels right, or it's compatible with the hero's character, the writer's attitudes or the tone of the book. The first-person voice best conveys the cheerful, wise-cracking, rough-diamond nature of a private eye, for example, the limited third person conveys a more distant, more cerebral atmosphere, and the multiple viewpoint is effective in novels that depend for effect on the reader knowing things the hero doesn't know.

Planning

Some writers blithely claim that they don't plan. They set their characters up in a promising situation and write to see what happens. Should we believe them? Envy them? Certainly if diverse characters in an exotic setting are allowed to engage with one another, then energy and momentum, arising out of conflict, are bound to get a story going.

But I wonder if it's necessarily a good idea for first-time crime writers to adopt this approach. I tried it with my first crime novel, *Kickback* (a method I'd used successfully many times in my 'literary' stories and novels, incidentally), and ended up with a messy manuscript—characters acting illogically, too many loose ends, and the plot full of holes, coincidences, and convenient but implausible actions. I threw it away and started again. Often I read published novels with some of these same faults—the result, I believe, of poor or inadequate planning. At the same time, I accept that many of the best crime novels I've read may not have been planned. Experienced writers tend to know when they are going off the rails and are able to start again, or cut or rework offending material.

Then again, crime fiction depends on carefully placed clues, unexpected twists, sustained suspense, mounting tension, moments of relief, turning points and hidden truths, and so I would argue that a certain amount of planning is advisable for your first crime novel.

As a result of my unhappy experience with *Kickback* I now spend several weeks planning the Wyatt crime novels before I begin to write them. There are certain things I know before I begin. I know the main character, the crime, and the rough 'formula' (Wyatt commits or attempts to commit a robbery, certain elements betray or oppose him, he gets his revenge. Formulas are also common in private-eye and police-procedural novels). There are many things I don't know, and so I invent them.

Other matters require research—how the electronic security systems in cars may be bypassed, for example. If my files don't produce the answers, I'll speak to experts. I want to avoid embarrassing mistakes (I learnt that the safe Wyatt carts away from the lawyer's office in *Kickback* would, in all probability, have been bolted to the floor) and skating over or conveniently avoiding technical details because they are too tricky. Often there will be points of information that govern the nature or direction of the story; these I research before I begin, or if they should crop up during the writing. Other questions may be answered in the final draft stage—the magazine capacity of a Browning pistol, for example. (Many writers make glaring errors about guns, incidentally, and gun-freak readers are likely never to read another of your books—which may not be a bad thing. Nevertheless, it's worth knowing that pistols are quite different from revolvers, for example, or that revolvers cannot be silenced effectively, and that certain handguns don't have safety catches.)

There are no right or wrong methods of planning. Some writers use a card system, marking characters, crimes, scenes and incidents on separate cards and shuffling them around as plot solutions, complications and contradictions arise. Others use a whiteboard, listing characters and their motives, goals and obstacles, and drawing lines to show intersections and outcomes. These kinds of mapping and diagramming can enable writers to view everything at a glance and avoid writing themselves into a corner.

Agatha Christie's method was to muse on plot and character for several weeks as she went about her day-to-day domestic affairs; then, when the story had taken shape to her satisfaction, she sat down and wrote it.

I don't have a whiteboard, find cards too fussy and am not confident of my ability to hold all the stages of a long work in my head. I prefer to plan on scrap paper, first making a few notes about the crime, the main characters and the broad plot stages, then over three or four weeks refining the storyline and fleshing it out with chapters, scenes and minor characters, revising and discarding endlessly until I have a plan that works.

I find it useful to trace the histories of my characters, reaching back into their pasts and projecting into their futures. This helps me not only to spot contradictions, coincidences, implausibilities and unnecessary material before it's too late, but also, more importantly, to identify where, when and how my characters *intersect* with one another.

I'll then muse on the ramifications of these intersections. For example: *I've introduced Sugarfoot as a foil to Wyatt in the first chapter, intending to drop him from the story now, but what if I were to have him brood on his grievances and later explode at a crucial point in the action?* If this new idea seems profitable, adding complexity and suspense to the story, I'll then go back and unravel and restitch the plan to accommodate it—but only if the seams don't show. I'd rather save a pleasing but unworkable idea, character or incident for my next book than let it spoil the one I'm working on.

Where possible in the planning stages I test the story: What does the hero want (his goal) and why (motive)? What—given his personality—is he prepared to do to achieve it? What is hindering him (character traits, external factors)? Would he trust this person, perform that action?

No matter which method you choose, one factor should remain constant—the close relationship between plot and character. Don't impose plot on the characters and don't indulge in character at the expense of a good plot.

Subplots

After sketching in the basic framework, I aim for a degree of complexity and density. I want readers to be involved and absorbed. I don't want them saying 'So what?'

Subplots add texture and depth to the main plot. One subplot is probably all that a short story can bear, but a novel may have more than one subplot. The easiest way to contemplate subplotting is to ask yourself: What person, event or complication might interfere with or enrich the main character or the main plot (note that subplots work best if they're not separate and arbitrary)? In 'Threshold' I worked in the theme of the young detective's anxiety about his capabilities, for he doesn't want to disappoint his boss, the clever, arrogant, impatient man who is in fact the killer. In my third Wyatt novel, *Deathdeal*, Wyatt finds himself working with someone he'd once loved, someone who'd deceived him. Can he trust her this time? Another subplot is his vulnerability: he's broke, can't rely on old friends, and is wanted by the law.

STRUCTURE

Basic shape

By tradition, crime novels and stories are linear in shape, involving set-up (the beginning), conflict (the middle) and resolution (the end). Novels, more so than stories, have a series of minor climaxes in the middle stage. These twists, turns, false resolutions, setbacks and complications have the effect of surprising readers, subverting their expectations, and delaying and thereby intensifying the effect of the final peak of tension, when all is revealed.

In my Wyatt novel *Paydirt*, I knew the main plotline before I started detailed planning. In the opening, Wyatt would fail in his solo attempt to steal a payroll and be forced to put a gang together and try other means. In the middle stages he would prepare for the robbery (not knowing what the reader knows, that other forces are conspiring against him), fail, and be forced to go on the run. At the end he determines who has cheated him and exacts his revenge. As you can see, each stage has its own set-up, conflict and resolution pattern.

My short story 'Threshold' started with an idea: a police inspector is in charge of the investigation into a murder that he himself has committed. I knew that if this were revealed at the end, the story would be a mystery. If it were revealed at the beginning, suspense would have to be generated by other means—readers wanting to know whether or not he would get away with it, for example. I wasn't confident that I could make the latter approach work in a story-length work and chose the first. But who would 'filter' the story to the reader? I decided on a young, inexperienced detective taking part in the investigation. He gathers information (the beginning), arrives at dead ends and false solutions and therefore starts to have doubts (the middle), and finally identifies his boss as the killer (the ending).

The beginning

Ideally, crime stories and novels open dramatically, arousing reader interest. An opening must deliver what it promises, however, and not simply startle for the sake of it. At some point in the opening chapter or scene, readers should gain a sense of the crime and the puzzle at the heart of the story, and an expectation of direction. The first chapter of a novel should also introduce the main character and end at a peak of tension or interest that will compel readers to turn to Chapter 2. The novel that opens with a large cast of characters, issues and details risks losing readers. Suspense and tension, in stories and novels, are maintained if readers' questions about the outcome are not answered until the end: don't give them too much too soon.

In the first chapter of *Kickback*, Wyatt, down on his luck, is forced to accept a small commission burglary for a fee, and to work with Sugarfoot, the inept but vicious and ambitious younger brother of the man who had hired him. At the end of the chapter the job has gone terribly wrong—the 'hook' that makes readers want to read on. Readers also know a little of Wyatt's character and capabilities, and have a sense of the appropriately clipped tone and cool mood of the book. Finally, I have also planted a slow-burning fuse: Sugarfoot. Full of grievances as a result of Wyatt's contemptuous treatment of him, Sugarfoot 'explodes' later in the book.

Remember, causality, however well buried, is a governing principle in crime fiction.

The middle

In the long middle stages of typical stories and novels, the main character attempts to resolve the issue set up in the beginning. He or she might make mistakes, uncover some keys to a mystery before hitting a brick wall, fail to act until it's too late, or be caught between various courses of action. Each situation gives promise of further situations, and tension remains unresolved.

In crime fiction in particular, a series of situations of doubtful outcome are presented progressively, building tension as the ending draws closer. At the same time, there may be an ever-present air of menace or suppressed violence, which may occasionally erupt into action.

Pacing is a vital consideration. A novel with an unrelenting headlong pace runs the same risk of alienating readers as a sluggish one. There should always be a sense of forward movement (where possible avoid digressions and inessentials, and don't rely overmuch on flashbacks), but at the same time it can be an effective device to vary scenes that are full of tension, action and drama with slower, more reflective ones.

Place your *surprises* carefully. A critical betrayal lies at the heart of *Kickback*: if revealed too soon, the remainder of the novel would have lacked tension; if revealed too late, it would have seemed tacked on. Try to anticipate what your readers want or expect at a certain point (action, a love scene, an explanation, a reconciliation, a betrayal) and either satisfy them or subvert their expectations with something unexpected (though plausible and logical in terms of character motivation and storyline).

Try to employ *delaying tactics*. Suspense lies in the reader asking: Whodunit? Who betrayed her? Will he get away with it? What happens next? Readers want to know, and your task is to make them want to know *badly*. Frustrate them a little, using unexpected reversals, partial or doubtful outcomes, pauses to consider related but less important themes. Get them to exercise their minds about the wrong problem, or a problem that's only tangential to the main one.

Finally, there should be a major *turning point* toward the end of the middle part of a story or novel. This is the point at which the main character begins to understand what is going on, and to take charge with a greater degree of confidence. It may be triggered by a hidden fact revealed, a mistake on the part of the villain, an obstacle overcome, a trap activated. It should not appear too late, but there may also be less vital (but no less surprising) turning points at the very end, when, for example, the apparent solution is only part of the real solution.

The end

By now you should be clear about the causality factors underpinning and governing your plot. If you have allowed them to play themselves out fully, hidden facts and themes will come to the surface, the killer will be unmasked, the missing person or loot found, a betrayal avenged, a degree of order restored. The outcome should not be tacked on for want of a more logical one, but should be the obvious extension of everything that has happened before it. It should not be clichéd, coincidental or convenient—the signs of a lazy or ill-prepared writer. It should not drag on too long, over-explain or introduce new material.

What types of causal factors might we find explained at the end? Ross Macdonald often let an event buried in the past (for example, a rich man concealing his paternity of an illegitimate child) trigger actions in the present. Minette Walters likes to explore the dark forces at work in a family, and Ruth Rendell often plots the gradual disintegration of the mind of an apparently normal person who has committed a crime. It's been said that murder can be explained by sex or money. Sex and money can mean a lot of things, however: love, hate, jealousy, rage, envy, fear, greed. People also kill to protect a loved one. They kill to protect themselves—their status, reputation, wealth, freedom.

You may find, when you write, that your plan is poorly conceived, inadequate, too restrictive or no longer appealing. If your instincts tell you to change direction, extend one character or downplay or drop another, or opt for a more exciting but still logical outcome, then you should not feel bound by the original plan. Simply test all changes in terms of the principles of causality and motive first.

Chapters and scenes

You have erected the framework; now you need to brick it in—with chapters and scenes in a novel; with scenes alone in a short story.

The end stage of my planning method is to list the probable chapters in the form of notes about the function (always one main function per chapter: for example, Wyatt learns who has betrayed him), content (that is, what happens, what is said, who is involved, where it takes place) and mood (for example, menace, bitter disappointment, relief). I stage them progressively, each chapter following logically from the pre-ceding chapter (unless interrupted by a 'meanwhile-back-at-the-ranch' chapter), and ending with a hook that implies the next stage or chapter.

Scenes are one of the main building blocks of stories and novels. Like chapters, they may be understood as stories in miniature, with characters, actions, a setting, speech, atmos-phere and a gradual build-up of tension leading to a resolu-tion. Like chapters, they are linked to scenes that precede and follow them.

Show, don't tell is a basic rule of fiction. If Bill is angry with the boss for being denied a promotion at work, don't simply state the fact but write a scene, using speech and action, that *shows* his anger. Of course, there are times when it's not possible or desirable to use a scene. A short expository passage will vary the pace and convey information quickly and effi-ciently. A summary between scenes can also be useful; for example, between the scene where Bill confronts his boss and the scene where he kills him, we might in a few lines describe how Bill gets the sack, declines into poverty and despair, and decides to seek his revenge.

A scene should be judged in terms of whether or not it develops or illustrates aspects of plot or theme. When writers rewrite, they often cut scenes that do not add to or support their intentions, or that unnecessarily repeat what is already known. They might also decide that a scene is too weak or uninteresting in itself and rework it as a summary.

How do you move your hero from A to B, or move from one stage of a story or novel to the next? Generally, if impor-tant events occur at both A and B, trivial details like travelling between the two points in a lift or taxi should be omitted—unless you wish to show your hero deciding on a course of action while riding in the taxi. You may also simply start a new chapter or scene with the hero already at B, or write something like: 'Later that afternoon . . .' In general, the purpose of a transition is to go forward in time or to a new location, or to introduce a new character. It should appear smooth and effortless.

Flashbacks

These are used to introduce background information at a certain point, information that would have slowed the unfolding of the plot if introduced earlier. Flashbacks tend to be past events replayed as a scene, reported in the narrative, or remembered in speech. They work best in novels; they tend to delay the action of a short story and so destroy tension. If the same information may be given in a better way, choose that over a flashback. If a flashback is unavoidable, it should be short, vivid and clearly defined.

Differences between short stories and novels

The obvious difference between stories and novels is length. Short, twist-in-the-tail stories may be as few as 1000 words long, magazine and anthology stories 3000 to 5000 words long on average but as long as 10 000 words, and novels anything from 50 000 to many hundreds of thousands of words. Length shouldn't be a problem at the outset: simply use as many words as necessary to do the job you've set out to do efficiently and effectively.

There are also differences in scope. Novels can be more relaxed, expansive and discursive than short stories. They tend to have more subplots, characters and setting changes, and cover a wider period of time. Short stories usually create a single impression and are more focused than novels. They tend to have few characters, a contained situation, limited settings and cover a small canvas. The problem for the writer of a crime short story is to introduce a puzzle quickly and solve it neatly and genuinely without relying on tricks and shortcuts. Novels usually explore many aspects of character, short stories only one, often revealed in a challenging situation.

COMMON FAULTS

Experienced writers redraft and refine their work several

times, often as they go along and always at the end. The following are the types of plot and structure faults that might need attention at the planning and rewrite stages:

- Coincidences and fortuitous encounters. These happen all the time in real life (a Melbourne detective on holiday in Perth once recognised and arrested a notorious criminal on the run from Victoria), but in fiction they seem contrived, an easy way out. They can be useful story *openings*, however.

- Detectives who don't detect but rely on luck and coincidence.

- Writing too much owing to a lack of focus. Sara Paretsky threw out 300 pages of *Tunnel Vision* because 'I was just kind of meandering and it just didn't have a shape.'

- Dead ends and sluggishness, owing to premature flashbacks, lack of a timeframe (e.g. an impending deadline or conflicting deadlines), lack of an essential character (for example, the failure of two characters to interact may be solved by introducing a third), or a reliance on introspection over action. (Raymond Chandler quipped that whenever he wrote himself into a corner he had a man walk through the door with a gun in his hand.)

- Unlikely but convenient oversights by your main character (would your experienced hero really forget to search the villain for a knife before tying her up?).

- An over-reliance on other characters to get your hero out of trouble. The new wave of crime writing by women rightly acknowledges the role of friendships, family and networking in women's lives, and private eyes have traditionally depended on reporters, police and public servants for information from time to time, but when it comes to the ultimate testing time, usually toward the end of the story, readers prefer their heroes to use their own wits and skills, not rely on the cavalry to ride to the rescue. In other words, the ending should be in your hero's hands.

- Heroes who are too brave, skilful and tough to be true. We like our heroes to be a little flawed and vulnerable; like us, good at some things, bad at others.

- Using tired old situations. In English manor-house mysteries, the detective gathers all the suspects together in one room and skilfully analyses motive, means and opportunity to unmask the murderer. Would a real murderer blithely stand by and let that happen?
- Foolish bravery. Private eyes are always going alone to meet strangers in isolated places at midnight. Are they mad?
- Too much padding (usually setting descriptions, character analysis, technical information, and 'instruction' in historical mysteries) at the expense of story.
- Secondary characters or plots that swamp the main character or plot.
- Awkward meshing of two fictional conventions: for example the traditional private eye novel with the lesbian coming-of-age novel.
- Withholding information that cannot logically be withheld: for example, the butler has been on stage all through the story but readers are not informed until the last scene that he has a wooden leg and must therefore be the killer.

Writers at Work

It's not unusual for writers' handbooks to make us feel anxious about our writing methods. I have just advised you to plan thoroughly. Here's what a number of experienced writers feel about planning:

Tony Hillerman never knows exactly where the plot is headed when he begins a book. He may know what the central crime is toward the end of the book, and what motivates it, but still not have worked out how to end the story.

John Grisham always starts with a plot idea, not a character, and writes 45–page outlines, with two paragraphs per chapter explaining precisely what will happen.

Charles Willeford believed that the reader may be privy to the criminal's knowledge but his protagonist shouldn't. He also advised against telegraphing plot intentions to the reader.

P. D. James spends about three years writing a novel, including eighteen months of plotting and planning before she starts to write.

James Lee Burke doesn't allow himself to see more than two scenes around the corner, and he revises endlessly: 'I feel you should be able to pop a page between your hands and nothing on it should rattle.'

Sara Paretsky began her first six books with the idea of a crime, then thought of a likely story and characters, but she started *Tunnel Vision* and *Guardian Angel* with characters, constructing both crimes and stories around them: '. . . a very scary way to write.'

Elmore Leonard doesn't plan but follows his instincts. He usually starts with an interesting character but isn't afraid to shine the spotlight on another character if the first one lacks interest or potential.

James Ellroy plans his novels thoroughly first. He wrote a 164-page outline of *White Jazz,* for example, and a 211-page outline of *L.A. Confidential,* admitting to a 15 per cent 'improvisation factor' in the 'fever-driven voice' of the final drafts.

Minette Walters's novel *The Scold's Bridle* grew out of a question: What would happen if all the members of a family tried to repress one another?

Perhaps all that matters is a point made by *Reginald Hill.* He believes that it's easy to mystify: 'The good mystery writer's real skill lies in clarification.'

Exercises

1. Here is an actual front-page summary of an item in a daily newspaper: 'A man paid a policeman posing as a hitman $10 000 to murder his former wife, the Magistrates Court was told yesterday.' As a crime writer, I can see sufficient drama and intrigue in this bare 'idea' to sustain a novel. It would not be necessary for me to know what really

happened—I would *imagine* an explanation. Let the writer in you speculate about this or a similar news story until characters, motives and a storyline emerge. For example: What are some plausible reasons why a man would want his wife killed? Who might be lurking behind the scenes? What if the policeman were corrupt? What if the hitman killed the wrong woman?

2. Once you have an idea of the story, decide how you are going to tell it. Where will you start? With discovery of the body or revelation of the mistake? Who is the protagonist and from whose point of view will the story be told? Devise a plot outline, either a step outline noting the significant incidents or a summary of the story. Use this as a map to refer to if you get lost. Once down on the ground you might find the story takes another, more interesting path.

5 CHARACTER

Minette Walters

The question I am asked more than any other is: Are your characters based on real people? The assumption seems to be that you can't create believable men and women unless you have first dissected your friends, acquaintances and relations and then reconstructed them on the written page under different names and thin disguises. Well, this may be true of some authors (although I have yet to meet one who's brave enough to admit to it), but it certainly isn't true of me. Every character I create is born out of my own imagination. And my imagination is stimulated through reading fiction and non-fiction, through watching films, stage-dramas and television, and through a constant diet of newspapers and current affairs broadcasts.

Of course I watch people—we all do—but I would never seek to reproduce anyone in their entirety in a story. Ultimately, my characters are a synthesis of a thousand experiences, a usefully eclectic memory and a lifetime of running the gamut of emotions from A (the abyss) to Z (the zenith). It is how an author uses this wealth of accumulated knowledge that makes him or her a successful writer of character. The freer your imagination, the more lifelike your characters. Take Dracula, who is one of the most fantastic of all fictional creations, and yet whose legend lives on because Bram Stoker breathed life into the living dead. Constrain your imagination and you and your characters will die of sheer boredom, because the process is a dynamic one and requires a constant dialogue between you and them as their story advances.

Nothing in the world fascinates me quite so much as human nature, our good deeds and our bad deeds, our individual ambitions which conflict all too regularly with the ambitions of our tribes, and our often vain attempts to prove to ourselves that mankind is intrinsically superior to the rest of the animal kingdom. We are in every respect a quite extraordinary evolutionary product, with traditions based on wonderful but different cultures, with a diversity of religions and philosophies that strive to bring us close to ideals of perfection, and with thousands of different languages and dialects. But against these structured backdrops, six billion of us across the planet have six billion individual personalities, six billion different physical characteristics and six billion sets of private thoughts.

It would be a very unimaginative author who could not embroider onto this amazing tapestry some realistic fictional people. Even the most phlegmatic among us must recognise that the permutations for character profiling are infinite.

Finding characters' voices (not to be confused with writing dialogue)

Creating characters means finding voices. In the end, it is not how people dress that differentiates them but how they think and speak. Identical twins may look alike but they won't have identical thoughts; just as ten soldiers wearing the same uniform will have ten different reasons for wearing it. It is not enough to imagine what your characters look like, what houses they live in or what jobs they do, you must talk to them and delve inside their heads to discover what is going on in there. Otherwise, they will be puppets on a stage with no independence of thought or action, and no reality beyond the purely visual.

There is, of course, an inherent paradox in that last sentence. You, the author, have invented these people. Their very existence depends on you; they have no freedom to do anything unless you allow it. However, in just the same way that good parents encourage their children to make lives of their own, so a good author must give his characters enough integrity to predict their own behaviour. Partially developed people have only partially developed aims and emotions, both in real life and in fiction, and they will behave unpredictably because they don't know who they are, why they are there, or what they are supposed to be doing. Nothing is less satisfying for a reader than to be presented with a muddled picture of unlikely people performing unlikely actions simply to push a plot forward.

Contrast Agatha Christie's two most famous creations; Miss Marple and Hercule Poirot. Miss Marple always seems to me to be a credible character: the inquisitive old lady living in a village, applying her knowledge of human nature in St Mary Mead to the greater world beyond because she understands that human motivation is much the same everywhere. She has a clear identity and a clear voice. She is the wise woman of folk literature, who derives her skills from a lifetime of watching the comings and goings of her neighbours. This is well demonstrated at the end of a short story published in 1932, near the beginning of Miss Marple's career. Her nephew, Raymond West, wonders how she made the leap between a Mr Hargraves, late of St Mary Mead, who, despite being respectably married, left all his money to a housemaid by whom he'd had five children, and a murderous travelling salesman, Mr Jones, who did away with his wife with the help of a servant girl.

> 'Well, Aunt Jane, this is one up to you,' [said Raymond]. 'I can't think how on earth you managed to hit upon the truth. I should never have thought of the little maid in the kitchen being connected with the case.'
> 'No, dear,' said Miss Marple, 'but you don't know as much of life as I do. A man of that Jones's type—coarse and jovial. As soon as I heard there was a pretty young girl in the house I felt sure that he would not have left her alone. It is all very

distressing and painful, and not a very nice thing to talk about. I can't tell you the shock it was to Mrs Hargraves, and a nine days' wonder in the village.'

'The Tuesday Night Club' (in *The Thirteen Problems,* first published by Wm. Collins, 1932)

Hercule Poirot, by contrast, is quite *in*credible. He is a buffoon whom we are told repeatedly is intelligent. He is depicted as a man of absurd affectations, who speaks smatterings of French interspersed with poor English and who is vain about his moustache and his 'little grey cells'. He is neither very funny nor very convincing. For a long time I avoided reading the Poirot stories because, for me, they were just an exercise in plot construction with a variety of wooden characters—Poirot himself, the idiotic Hastings and the even more idiotic Inspector Japp, all of whom were just pale imitations of Sir Arthur Conan Doyle's Sherlock Holmes, Dr Watson and Inspector Lestrade.

'*Mon ami*, Hastings!' [Poirot] cried. '*Mon ami*, Hastings!'

And, rushing forward, he enveloped me in a capacious embrace. Our conversation was incoherent and inconsequent. Ejaculations, eager questions, incomplete answers, messages from my wife, explanations as to my journey, were all jumbled up together.

'I suppose there's someone in my old rooms?' I asked at last, when he had calmed down somewhat. 'I'd love to put up here again with you.'

Poirot's face changed with startling suddenness. '*Mon Dieu!* But what a *chance épouvantable.* Regard around you, my friend.'

The Big Four (first published by Wm. Collins, 1927)

Although both characters have been interpreted widely for film and television, Miss Marple in her various guises usually retains her dignity and wisdom, while Poirot, despite being clever enough to think his way though problems (in the manner of Holmes), invariably becomes a figure of fun. Not until David Suchet's inspired portrayal of the character for television did Poirot achieve any sort of serious substance, for Suchet translates Poirot into a caring man, who is less concerned about voicing his own brilliance and more concerned for others' pain, and who has enough wry humour to poke a little fun at his own vanities. I would argue that this is *not* the character Agatha Christie invented, but a logical extension of it, and has resulted in the little Belgian finally receiving an authentic voice.

So how do you set about finding these voices? Well, as in everything else, there are probably a hundred ways of doing it and you have to choose a method that suits you. Your aim is to establish within your head people of such clear identities and personalities that when you put them on the page they virtually write themselves. This may take time, but it's time well spent. I tend to play with ideas on character for several weeks before I begin a story. This may involve writing them down and trying them out, or letting them lie in my subconscious while I work on something else. But, as I said, this is a dynamic process. Your characters will react with each other as they come together in the story; they will evolve and develop through their relationships with each other, just as we do in real life. The trick is to try to understand them well enough to know which way they are likely to jump.

(This doesn't always work. I've had to alter plots in the past when it's become clear to me that characters *would* not or *could* not do what I wanted.)

John, Michael, Mary and Hannah: A case in point

You will usually begin with your principal characters. Let's say you are looking for four of them—two men and two women. You don't know yet what their names are going to be but we will call them John and Michael, Mary and Hannah. Depending on the plot you have chosen, be it fully fledged or still in embryo, you will know roughly what, if any, relationships exist between these four protagonists. For the sake of argument, let's say that John and Mary are married, Michael is Hannah's brother, and Hannah, whose husband has been murdered, is having an affair with John.

It is irrelevant at this stage how Hannah's husband was killed, who the killer is or how you intend to work through to the eventual denouement. What is important is to establish clear reasons why any one of these four might have been driven to see murder as a solution, and to do that you must examine the pain/anger/jealousy they have suffered as a result of Hannah's marriage to the dead man and Mary's marriage to John.

This is the beginning of your own dialogue with these imaginary people.

Does Hannah feel any regret for her dead husband? Why has she been having an affair with John? Because she's promiscuous? Because she hated her husband? Because she felt unloved? Why was John having the affair? Because his marriage to Mary has broken down? Because Hannah is just another trophy? What was going on between Michael and his dead brother-in-law before the murder? Were they partners in a business venture? How long has Mary known Hannah? Does she know about the affair? Are she and Hannah friends?

If I were writing this story, the characters would begin to take shape along these lines:

Hannah projects herself as a victim. She has been used by two men, her husband and John, and the net result of both relationships is a growing despair. Like anyone who is searching for love, she appears to be deeply confused about how love demonstrates itself. Is it through sex with John? Or through the tearful love that her husband offered her between his drunken bouts of jealous rage? Her despair is exacerbated because she and Mary are friends, and, when her initial infatuation for John dies, she seeks to extricate herself without Mary ever finding out what she's done. But she learned shortly before her husband's death that he already knew and was threatening to make the fact public. How far does the image she projects reflect the real Hannah?

John has long since lost any affection for his wife but remains with her because it suits him to do so. (Perhaps she owns the house, or earns more money, or he doesn't want her to have control of his children.) He plays the field with any women who are interested but has few feelings for them until he becomes involved with Hannah and falls for the despair and the vulnerability that are her trademark. He is more accustomed to forceful women (mother, wife), and the appeal that Hannah makes to his dormant protectiveness is powerful, particularly when she comes to him, bruised and battered, after a row with her husband. But how long would this sort of defenceless woman hold his attention? Does he really like clinging women?

Michael understands his sister better than anyone else because he grew up with her. He believes that the image she projects is very different from the reality because he knows Hannah to be more manipulative than anyone recognises. (*Why? What happened in the past to persuade him of this?*) However, he also knows that her husband is a pathologically jealous man, who knew about the affair and who is capable of extreme violence. Michael's position is complicated by a financial bond with the dead man (business? debt?) so his brother-in-law's death would be convenient. How far does the family talent for manipulation extend? Is the image that Michael projects as false as his sister's? And does he dislike her enough to push the guilt on to her?

Mary will always be the most tantalising of the four characters. She appears, after all, to have the least reason for wishing Hannah's husband dead. She doesn't like her own husband but she does nothing to get rid of him. She undoubtedly knows about the affair because the dead man will have told her, if only to revenge himself on John. So what motivates her? It *must* be self-interest, because that is the most basic of all human instincts. My own suspicion is that she has two teenage children towards whom she is extremely protective (perhaps they've given a point to her life that was never there before—*N.B. some interesting resonances here in terms of John's protectiveness towards Hannah*). I think Mary has already consulted a solicitor with a view to divorce, has learnt the unpalatable truth that divorce will result in her children having the right to choose which parent they would prefer to live with, and is afraid that one of them, at least, won't choose her. (*Which one? An area of conflict—adolescent turmoil, made worse by John's waywardness and Mary's over-protectiveness. More resonances with what happened between Michael and Hannah during* their *childhood.*) Only prolonged and proven drink/drug addiction or a criminal conviction would lead a judge to award sole custody to Mary. In view of the fact that Hannah's husband, before his death, was threatening to expose the scandal of all their double lives to the respectable community they live in, does Mary hate John enough to set him up as the fall guy for the murder and so get him off her back for good?

Anyone who has read my stories will know that these preliminary sketches are bare bones only. After all, these four people haven't even met each other yet. So, like Jack Blakeney, my artist in *The Scold's Bridle* who paints character in colour-coded abstract, I will 'go on now for weeks, working layer on layer, attempting . . . to build and depict the complexity of the human personality.' But the point is, the voices have begun.

As yet, they are muted because there's still far too much that we don't know. How old are they? How do they speak to each other? What sort of backgrounds do they come from? Are their names really John, Mary, Michael and Hannah? How much of themselves is hidden?

Off the top of my head, I'd say Mary has the potential to hide more of her real self than the others, but she may still emerge as the only honest character in this story. Hannah's hidden self may be a double bluff. I'm tempted to think she really *is* a vulnerable woman who, in this modern age, can't admit it and complicates everything by persuading her brother she has far more control than she actually does. And who's to say Michael's telling the truth about Hannah? He claims she's manipulative. But does anyone else? Surely this is a case of the pot calling the kettle black. And what of John? He must be an attractive man because he persuades women into bed with remarkable ease, yet he cares nothing for them. This is a dangerously egocentric personality, and all the more intriguing because of it. Barbara Peters, the highly respected owner of The Poisoned Pen Bookshop in Scottsdale, Arizona, argues that egocentricity (i.e. seeing the world with yourself at its centre) may be a character trait common to murderers. It's a very selfish mentality that takes the life of another in order to make things better for itself.

However, if I explore these people any further, I shall end up writing their story and, sadly for them, they *were* just examples plucked from the air.

Secondary characters and their function

Like the extras on a stage or in a film, your secondary characters are there to give the story life and body. Of course you could write about four people only. Jean-Paul Sartre's play *Huis Clos* portrays three people shut in a room together. As the play unfolds, they come to recognise that they have died and gone to hell, and that for the rest of eternity they are destined to be closeted together in this one small room, repeating the same boring conversations over and over again. But most of us lack Sartre's genius, and secondary characters are useful.

In terms of a crime story, they serve to point the finger of suspicion at the various protagonists and, as in any novel, help in the dynamic process of character evolution through what they can reveal. Because I try to give all my characters weight, though clearly some will have more weight than others, I find it important to see where and how my secondary characters fit into the scheme of things.

If we revert briefly to our embryonic story, then we know that there are already three extras in this plot: John and Mary's two children and the solicitor she consulted about her divorce. In addition, there may be a lover from John's past; and his mother, the strong-minded woman who brought him up—does she have a role in this? As a living presence or a dead one? There are also Michael and Hannah's parents, who must carry some responsibility for the fact that one or both of their children feel it necessary to hide their true self behind a facade. For example, how have they contributed to their daughter's disastrous marriage?

If the story is set in a village or small community, then neighbours become important; if it is centred on a place of work, then colleagues become important. In the end, it is what the secondary characters reveal about the protagonists that keeps the suspense going, for they, being less directly affected by the murder, will probably be the most objective. I am interested in the fact that truth is always relative (i.e. each of us is highly selective about what we choose to see and believe), so I try to place my secondary characters into strongly defined backgrounds with some sort of indication of the values they hold. Then the reader has a chance of deciding how valid their opinions are.

A good example of this is Sister Bridget in *The Sculptress*. Her credentials are impeccable. She is a nun, a convent school headmistress, she was one of Olive Martin's teachers, and she visits Olive regularly in prison. We should be able to have faith in what she says both about Olive and about the murders of Olive's sister and mother. Certainly, we feel that she is *trying* to be as honest as she can. However, she admits that she has never liked Olive, and this may or may not colour her perceptions of what Olive might have done.

Or, as Anne Cattrell reflects in *The Ice House*: 'Could reality be quantified, Anne wondered, any more than truth? To say yes to such a question from such a man would be a betrayal. His capacity for understanding was confined by his prejudices.'

The investigating character

This is most commonly a policeman or a detective and is often a series character. But it can, of course, be anyone you like. In *The Sculptress*, the investigator is an author. In *The Scold's Bridle*, the job is shared between a detective sergeant, approaching retirement and hoping for promotion, and a female doctor who seeks to fend off her own arrest after her patient is murdered.

In many ways, the investigating character is the least constrained of all the characters. He/she can go anywhere, talk to anyone, ask anything. He can also try to interpret what is going on as it's happening. Whether or not the interpretation is correct is immaterial: it's one way of heightening suspense.

If you choose to write in the first person, as many crime authors do, then you can add to this investigating-character equation all the terrible uncertainties, fears and weaknesses that any normal person experiences when faced with things they don't understand. You do, however, limit yourself in terms of action to what can be relayed through one person's eyes.

For all sorts of reasons, I have deliberately avoided writing a series, largely because I relish my freedom to write who I want when I want, but for those who choose series characters, there is a different kind of freedom. You already have a protagonist who is sharply defined and well rooted in place and time. You know how he/she thinks before you even begin your story, and you know how he/she will react in any given situation. This is a bonus. Where I am feeling my way, the series-character writer marches forward with confidence because they are hand in hand with someone who already exists.

I offer a small caveat on the creation of series characters. Do not encumber your first novel with minute details about the character's life because you will be stuck with them forever, and you may well wonder what on earth you can say about him/her in the future that will be as interesting as the character's first appearance. Be vaguer than you feel you should because, as the series progresses, you may not want his/her birthday to be June 27, or his/her dog to be called Fido, or his/her mother to be an alcoholic. It's a tragedy for readers when authors become so bored with their over-defined characters that they send them hurtling over the Reichenbach Falls just to get rid of them.

The murder victim

If, as I do, you murder your victim in the first few pages, then that character can only be depicted through what other people say. The dead are always silent. This area fascinates me, simply because I doubt anyone's ability to 'know' another person when much of the time we don't even 'know' ourselves. There is a visual parallel of this in the reversed reflection of the mirror. Unless we appear regularly on television or in the cinema, the only picture we have of our faces is an inverted one.

However, the victim is in many ways the central character in a crime story. Without his/her death there can be no action, so it is very important to bring that person back to life through the eyes of those who knew him/her. Unless you are writing about a stranger murder—one where the victim is unknown to the killer—then the motive for the victim's death must lie somewhere in the victim's personality and/or history and/or relationships. If we return to John, Mary, Michael and Hannah, clearly it is the dead man and how he affected all their lives that will be the driving force of the story. Why did one of them hate him and fear him enough to kill him?

You may choose to depict your victim alive before his/her death, as Ngaio Marsh did in most of her books. Then the emphasis of the story shifts because the victim can speak for him/herself and you are setting up clear reasons in advance why various people might want to do away with this often unpleasant person. I use diary extracts in *The Scold's Bridle* as a way of giving the victim (Mathilda Gillespie) a chance to speak for herself. This means she can explain in her own words why she was a victim, and her explanation is very different from the largely simplistic motives that the police uncover.

The murderer

Unless, like Patricia Highsmith in her Tom Ripley books, you make the murderer/psychopath your lead character, your murderer will simply be one of the many people featured in the story. Only at the end does he/she become in any way extraordinary, and then it's up to you how that person chooses to deal with the shock of exposure. There are some excellent non-fiction books on the market which contain interviews with convicted murderers, and they give insights into the kind of thought processes that go on at the time of the murder, the arrest and the trial. They are worth reading if for no other reason than that they show how like the rest of us most murderers are!

Character and dialogue

How your characters speak is of such fundamental importance to the development of their personas that a few hints on dialogue may be appropriate here. You can, of course, develop your plot through speech just as successfully as you can develop your characterisation, so dialogue must be tight and to the point. The mistake that some authors make is to take it down to a bare minimum, with the result that full stops are the only punctuation and sentences are lucky to reach five words in length. But this kind of dialogue is the preserve of film and television, where paragraphs of speech mean the camera must focus too long on one person, and where the pace slows when the actor or actress cannot produce enough facial expressions to keep the watcher's interest.

To a certain extent, the same is true of a novel—waffle and spoken padding become tiresome—but to attempt to read a book where every character is allowed to deliver only one sentence at a time is a breathtaking experience. The pace becomes so rapid, and the characters so shallow, that you might as well be on the receiving end of machine-gun fire. As in everything else, writing dialogue is a balancing act. You don't want to underdo it and you don't want to overdo it. Page-long paragraphs of speech are probably overdoing it. One-liners all the way through are probably underdoing it. The more natural you can make it, bearing in mind that you must impose some stylistic discipline—you should not allow a character to repeat the same word five times in a piece of dialogue any more than you would repeat it in a paragraph of descriptive prose—the better it will be.

Naming your characters

My only advice on this is to be comfortable with the names you choose. If you're happy with exotic names, then use exotic names, but don't rely on a name to give your character anything extra. In the end, it is your portrayal of the people you write about that matters and if your hero/heroine is sympathetic then it doesn't matter whether you've called him/her: Maximilian de Winter/Mrs de Winter, Sydney Carton/Miss Manette, Robin Hood/Marian, Mr Darcy/Elizabeth Bennett, Rhett Butler/Scarlett O'Hara. (My own favourites among that little lot are Sydney Carton, from *A Tale of Two Cities*, by Charles Dickens; Mr Darcy and Elizabeth Bennett, from *Pride and Prejudice*, by Jane Austen; and the first Mrs de Winter, *Rebecca*, who sprang from Daphne du Maurier's amazing genius. And they all have such ordinary names.)

Memorable characters

Many successful books have been written on plot alone, with only the barest nod towards character creation and development. The most obvious examples are the various types of formula thriller, where action is everything and the characters fall into two or three stereotypical categories—the gung-ho, brave hero; his shadowy, sometimes sadistic, always rich, evil counterpart; and the pale heroine who clings to the hero when he rescues her. They sell and they make money, so it's certainly not a prerequisite of success to take the trouble to build and explore the people you write about.

However, the books that endure and continue to sell long after the authors are dead are the ones whose characters take such a powerful hold on readers' imaginations that they seem to exist in their own right, simply because everybody knows them: Philip Marlowe (created by Raymond Chandler); Emma Bovary (created by Gustave Flaubert); Ebenezer Scrooge (created by Charles Dickens); Lady Macbeth (created by William Shakespeare); Dr Jekyll and Mr Hyde (created by Robert Louis Stevenson). These people were portrayed so perfectly that we know them as well as we know Winston Churchill or Marilyn Monroe. We can even cite them in conversation because they've become known points of reference, as in 'He's a real Jekyll and Hyde.'

Certainly, for me, a large part of the thrill of being an author lies in the relationship I develop with the people I write about. After a while, they can become very real and, like the actor who is playing Hamlet, I have to school myself to 'drop out of character'. One day a poor friend of mine telephoned to give me the latest tearful account of her ongoing break-up with the man in her life, and I was so caught up in a confrontational scene I was writing between two women in *The Scold's Bridle* that I told her to pull herself together and be glad she'd got rid of him so easily. In the circumstances, this was hardly the most tactful response, and it was six months before she spoke to me again. I expect Flaubert had similar problems when he created Emma Bovary. When asked who the character was based on, he always said: 'Madame Bovary is myself.'

The aim of any author must surely be to draw his readers into the fantasy world he has created and then invite them to participate. So I want my readers to feel involved, I want them to love, I want them to fear, I want them to experience anguish. Ultimately, I want them to turn the last page and regret that the story has finished.

And they won't do that unless they have heard the voices, too!

EXERCISES

1. A name is often the reader's first introduction to a character. The name Wilfred creates a different mental image from the name Kylie. This first exercise is a visualisation and would work most effectively if you could prerecord it or have someone talk you through it.

   Write a name, the first name that comes into your head, in the top left-hand corner of a sheet of paper. Close your eyes and see the name on the white background. Now imagine that this is a name tag on a piece of clothing. In your mind's eye you can see this garment quite clearly. Now visualise the person wearing this garment and follow them as they move along the street. How do they walk? Do they stride confidently, are they hesitant? Follow them into the place they call home. What is it like? Are there other people there? What is the furniture like, the atmosphere? Put on the character's clothes, put on their skin and go inside their mind. How do they view the world? What is the thing they most want, and the thing they most fear? Come back from this journey and write down your impressions of the character.

2. Character profile. Much of the information in your character profile will never appear in your story, but a comprehensive profile allows you to know your characters and how they will act/react in a given situation.

   What is your character's date of birth? The date of birth will tell you not only the character's age but what influenced them during their formative years. Someone who grew up during the Depression will have a different world view from someone who was young in the flower-power 1960s, or the 'greed is good' 1980s.

   What was their position in the family? The responsible, 'bossy' eldest child? The youngest, the 'baby' of the family? The only child who grew up to be the lone operator, the private detective?

   Finally, whether you believe in astrology or not, what is the character's star sign? This will give you an instant character profile.

3. Put your character in a situation, e.g. coming to see a private investigator, being interviewed by the police. If the character is a spoilt brat, what kinds of things do they say and do that will lead the reader to this conclusion? Show, don't tell.

6 DIALOGUE

J.R. Carroll

Real and realistic dialogue

Ernest Hemingway once said something to the effect that when he wrote his short stories in Paris cafes during the 1920s he could labour for long periods over a phrase or a single word, trying to make it perfect, but once the people—he called them people, not characters—began speaking to one another, he would have trouble sharpening his pencils fast enough to keep up with them. It was dialogue more than anything that brought the story to life and made the people in it seem real to him, as if they were sitting at the next table and he could overhear snatches of their conversation. Of course Hemingway was famous for his direct speech, which is characteristically taut, lean and forceful, yet when you read his dialogue you can't help thinking that there's something curiously oblique and inferential about it, that people really *don't* speak that way, that Hemingway was inventing a kind of spoken language rather than putting it down exactly the way it was. Ironically, that same style, with its Transatlantic mixture of tough, slangy, repetitious bar-and-gym talk and faintly effeminate English genteelisms like 'certainly', 'frightfully', 'truly', and 'grand'—the hallmarks of his youthful success in *The Sun*

Also Rises and *A Farewell to Arms*—eventually became a favourite subject for lampooning, alongside the excessive bravado and melodrama of his later, inferior, work.

Hemingway did not write crime stories—although stylistically *To Have and Have Not*, 'The Killers', 'Fifty Grand' and a number of others come close; in fact, a contemporary critic suggested that without him there would have been no 'gangster fiction' as we know it—but the point about the importance of getting the dialogue right still applies when discussing that genre, perhaps to an even greater degree. Crime novels, more so than mainstream fiction, stand or fall on the strength of it. Not surprisingly, Elmore Leonard, a crime writer with a stranglehold on dialogue, says he learned his skills from reading Hemingway. In crime fiction you need force, immediacy, a vivid sense that these things are being said *now*, in front of you, and for the first time. Most authors can write reasonable descriptive prose, but the true test comes when the talk begins. Try reading it aloud. If it sounds wrong, if it makes you cringe to hear your own spoken words, there's a big problem. And you can't cover for weak or unconvincing dialogue. People say, 'But dialogue is so damned *hard*!', to which I can only answer that they are not eavesdropping enough. I don't believe for a minute that someone with no ear for it can ever be *taught* to write dialogue—just as a tone-deaf person will always be hopeless at music—but if the raw material is there, together with a willingness to become a slave to this most demanding field and to immerse oneself in the works of successful practitioners, then there is some point to the exercise.

Real speech is invariably fractured, repetitive, dull and cliché-ridden. People don't usually speak whole sentences, they are ungrammatical and they use a lot of 'ums' and 'ahs'. In effect the writer has to doctor ordinary language to bring it up to scratch. This applies especially to the crime writer, since criminals tend not to be educated. Their speech is often primitive, coarse in the extreme and full of slang and colourful expressions. When writing dialogue you need to give the flavour of crimespeak, but if you reproduce it word for word you'll end up with dialogue that is dull, repetitive, disjointed, or even incomprehensible. I have read transcripts of bugged conversations between drug dealers, and they consist mostly of swear words, tortured syntax, contradictions, repetitions, the word 'mate', clumsily coded references to a third party, hesitations, large slabs of garbled, inarticulate mutterings and ejaculations that make no sense at all. Every second word is an obscenity, and you just couldn't do it that way in a book. It must be remembered that hard crims live an extreme, outsider's existence in which everything is done to excess. In Hemingway's phrase, they live their lives 'all the way up', and it shows in the way they talk. Intensity, edginess, fatalism, concealment, paranoia, amorality, gallows humour and an us-against-them attitude—it's all there in their speech, much of which is learned inside courts and prison walls. In the case of police, their delivery is invariably stilted and formal when they are dealing with the public, but at the coalface they might present a different image altogether.

As a crime novelist of the so-called hard-boiled or realistic school, the question I am most asked is, 'How do you make it so authentic? You must hang out a lot with cops, ride in their squad cars. You must spend a lot of time with homicide detectives, listening to the way they talk . . .' That kind of thing. My answer is always, disappointingly from their point of view, No. None of the above. Nor do I rub shoulders with crims in low dives. I do practically no research of any kind. So how do I make it real? It's a good question.

I don't know.

I just write it the way I think it should be written, and it usually *sounds* right to my ear. If it doesn't I get rid of it. It's no good forming emotional attachments to a particular phrase or sentence, even if you think it's the most wonderful piece of work ever created. If in doubt, don't agonise—throw it out. But back to the question: How do I make it real? How does anyone?

I've read a lot of crime books and followed a lot of court cases. I'm actually *interested* in crime, which helps. I listen. I remember a lot of detail. Little things stick in my mind. If I overhear something I store it away for future reference. For example, once I was walking past a pub towards my car, and there were two men in shorts standing on the footpath having a conversation. One looked fairly respectable, the other—well, his legs were festooned with tattoos and his face looked as if he'd been verballed a few times too often. The respectable one said, 'Coming in for a drink?' and his mate said, 'No. I don't want to run into any heads I used to know years ago.' Those words spoke volumes, and I never forgot them. About three years later, I used that exact line in a book called *Out of the Blue.*

So, in general, that's how I work—paying attention, being receptive, picking up bits and pieces, getting a *feel* for the way people who are going to inhabit my books might express themselves. Sometimes no words are needed to make meanings crystal clear. There was the time I was in a pub talking to a man I'd just met. He had strong opinions and, it seemed to me, first-hand knowledge of what was happening on the local crime front. One thing led to another, then I mentioned the name of a certain villain who had been off the scene for a while. He didn't respond immediately, but slowly and silently allowed a thick gob of spittle to fall from his mouth. That was all.

I haven't used that one yet. But I will.

Revealing character through dialogue

Now let's examine some of the more specific considerations in the use of dialogue. For instance, what are its functions? We already know from Hemingway that dialogue makes writing come alive, but what does this really mean in practical terms?

In the first place, dialogue is a key to revealing a person's distinguishing features, their attitudes and social background. A retired police commissioner is likely to have different speech patterns from a fifteen-year-old street kid. It is essential when writing a crime novel to delineate the characters sharply. It's no good having them all sound and behave alike, even if they are all roughly of a kind. It's true that action is character, but so too is speech. People *are* the way they sound; they are defined by their use of language. It is infinitely preferable, and more interesting, for characters to reveal themselves through their own words than to have them passively described in the third person. By way of illustration, here's a passage from a book of mine, *Tropic of Fear*, about a criminal-turned-informer, Don Bartholomew, who's hiding out in North Queensland. He comes home one day and finds a man he barely knows, Carl Collins, and a strange woman in his kitchen. The woman is smoking a cigarette. What's going on? Collins offers Don a can of beer from his own fridge—an unnerving situation. He angrily tells them to get out, but then another man emerges from the hallway, half naked and carrying a Magnum handgun.

'How do, mate,' the man said.

'Jeff.'

Jeff Woodhouse sloped in and took the can from Collins' hand.

'How long now? Ten years?' he said, then drank.

'At least that.' Don did not like the extra dimension now with the gun brought into it, and went carefully. 'What's the story, Jeff?' he asked more reasonably.

'Story? Well, it's complicated, like Carl said. Let's just call this a flying visit. We got into a jam, see, and who better than an old mate to put you up?' He looked at Don a moment, then laughed explosively. 'Jesus. Should see your fuckin' face! Looks like you just let one go with lumps in it!' He laughed some more, whacking Don's chest with his left hand, the one holding the can. Don stood his ground, not impressed with the beer splashed over his shirt. His eyes returned to the .357 and Woodhouse seemed to notice it himself for the first time.

'This worry you?' he said, and placed the gun butt-first in Don's hand. 'No need. What's mine's yours, remember?' Looking into Don's eyes at close quarters he said to the others, 'This man and me were brothers once. In for a penny, in for a pound. No favour too great. Right, Don?'

'That's how it was.' He put the gun on the table. Things unwound just a notch inside him.

'And you've already met the old girl, Vicky here.'

'Yes.'

'She's in the club, as you can see. Sorry I wasn't here myself for the introductions, but I was dead to the world, mate. Which reminds me. Don't mind sleeping on the couch for a while, do you? We've kind of taken over the bedroom.'

So the scene is set, with Don the host–hostage. From this exchange we know that Woodhouse, not Don, is in control. Woodhouse is a confident, intimidating presence. He appropriates the can from Collins. He switches suddenly from raucous humour to concentrated earnestness, gives a hint of veiled menace—here is a man capable of extreme mood swings. He hands Don the gun, testing their old friendship. Obviously he knows Don well enough to take that chance. And the offhand way in which he tells Don that they've taken over the bedroom makes it plain that the issue is non-negotiable. So while not much actually *happens* here, character is revealed and the dynamics of the situation are put in place. There are also strong overtones of tension, with a violent outcome very much on the cards should the 'guests' wear out their welcome.

Here's another passage, again in a domestic context. This is from *No Way Back*, about a somewhat unhinged detective, Dennis Gatz, who arrives home one morning from an all-night stake-out, during which he shot the wrong man, to find a removal van outside the house and his wife packing up and leaving. He blocks her passage and demands to know what the hell's going on.

'There's nothing to discuss, Dennis. It's all been said, many times. Let me through, please.'

'Put the box down. Tell me what the fuck you're doing.' His voice has dropped. A trembling fist wants to smash her in the mouth. He's on the brink.

'I've already told you.' But she knows him, knows his frame of mind too well. And puts down the box.

'Now look,' he says, 'I just come home from work, all night on the fuckin' job, shot a guy, Lauren, killed this cunt—'

'Dennis!' She's got him by the arms now, a steadying grip. He's in tears, starting to unravel before her. This is something else she knows all about. 'Listen! I'm sorry if something bad's happened, but it's not my problem any more. Do you hear? Not my problem. Now come on!' she shouts. 'Get a grip, will you? Face reality! Jesus.'

Now she lets go, withdraws. He's marginally calmer.

'Reality?' He wipes a jacket sleeve over his face. 'What's that? Tell me.'

What we have here is a compressed sketch of Dennis, together with an understanding of the kind of marriage Lauren has had to put up with. He is neurotic, job-obsessed, emotionally and physically volatile, blind to his shortcomings as husband and human being. He is exactly the kind of dysfunctional individual any sensible woman would want to leave. And when he asks what reality is, he's not just being facetious or obtuse—he really needs to know. His professional and home life are now in tatters, the future looks grim. It's as if he has fallen off the planet and is tumbling helplessly through space. And this is just the *start* of the book.

Character needs to be delineated in any kind of novel, but the exigencies of crime fiction demand a strict, disciplined approach that doesn't allow for the luxury of teasing out quirks and foibles and building a picture of someone at a nice, relaxed pace. You must get on with it, get the story rolling. You must present characters who are already fully formed and physically recognisable, and the best way of doing this is to let them reveal themselves. Try to think of Philip Marlowe without his dry, self-deprecating witticisms, Ruth Rendell's Inspector Wexford without his bluff, old-fashioned observations on modern life, or TV's Inspector Morse without his arrogance— they all merge into one. In other words, they have no distinctive voice or presence. It is those particular mannerisms, verbal and otherwise, that make individuals interesting. In *Catspaw*, I introduced a character called Alfie Meehan, an ex-jockey cum hitman who confronts Don Bartholomew about his early release from prison, correctly believing that Don must have done a deal with the cops. Alfie is a deadly little man, and Don has to tread warily through the following interrogation:

'You wouldn't be a copper, would you, Don?' Alfie said.

'Give it a go, would you, Alf? If that's what you think, you're way off beam.'

'I hope that what you say is true, Don. Because if you're

feeding me bullshit and you turn out to be a copper, I'll kill you just like that.'

'That won't be necessary. You're worrying about nothing, Alf.'

'Tom Coutts thinks you're a copper. He told me that at the restaurant.'

'That means fuck-all, Alfie. I couldn't give a shit what Tom Coutts thinks. Is that why you got me here?'

'Don't get all worked up, mate. I don't necessarily agree with Coutts. But he has got a good nose for coppers. I just wanted to hear what you had to say about it, that's all. Maybe Tom's right and maybe he's wrong. It's only that I have a very suspicious nature where my own skin is concerned. You can understand that, can't you, mate? Wouldn't you want to ask a few questions if you were in the same position?'

'Coutts has got it all wrong. There's no way I'm a copper, Alfie. You can forget that.'

Alfie thought about it. It was a warm day, but he had on a wool jacket, and Don knew he would be carrying a .22 pistol. He had used a .22 on all his victims.

From this we learn that Alfie, who is wanted in every state, is cold, cunning and devious. Not a man to waste words, he comes straight out with his suspicions to get Don off balance. Few people can lie convincingly when asked a direct question, and Don can't be sure whether he has passed the test or not. The threat to Don's life is established, and it hangs over him for the rest of the book. The reader, like Don, is going to be on the lookout for Alfie.

Providing plot information

In providing plot information, dialogue has the advantage of presenting it in a lively and colourful way. The information is also placed in context and is more credible, since it flows naturally from the characters and story rather than being tediously paraded to the reader as a list of facts. For example, towards the end of *No Way Back*, Dennis Gatz is listening and looking via a keyhole while the following conversation takes place between a psychopath named Sean and a bent cop, whose identity Dennis doesn't yet know:

'Calm down,' Sean said, and produced something from the desk drawer. 'Here. Choke on that for the time being.' He tossed what looked like a roll of notes, and the second man caught it. 'Call that a down payment.'

'How much is there?' the mate said. Who owned that fucking voice?

'Ten grand. Put it in your pocket.'

The man did so and said, 'I could use a fuckin' drink.'

'Well have a fuckin' drink then. You know where it is.'

The man moved completely out of sight and Dennis heard a steel cabinet open and a bottle clink. Then the man's back returned as a blurred edge to the keyhole. Dennis saw the bottle, White Horse, being poured into a glass.

'What about you?' the man said. Ah yes. That's who. Well well.

'Why fuckin' not,' Sean said, and accepted a drink. 'Just one of these brings five,' he said, looking at the cigar boxes. 'And we've got fuckin' five hundred coming. What does that work out at?'

There was silence as the other man had trouble with his sums.

'Is it two and a half million?' he said.

Sean laughed. 'Fuckin' oath it is. That's six noughts each after paying off the German end.'

'Can you get rid of that much of it?'

'Can I. It'd disappear without a trace in the weightlifting game alone, mate. Without a fuckin' trace.'

'The punters won't like that,' Gavin Spicer sniggered. 'They'll want results.'

'They'll get results. So will we. Everybody wins in this. You'll be able to give the game away.'

'I want to. I will. I been fuckin' lucky a long time. When's delivery again?'

'Two weeks tomorrow. Remember it's the *Dortmund*. Just make sure you fix things with the customs bloke, right? That's all you've got to do, that one thing.'

'That's no problem. He's sweet. Sling him something, five I guess. That'll do him.'

So it goes on, with the reader being given information at the same time as Dennis. Revealing facts in that way, from the point of view of the main character, reassures the reader and allays suspicion that the author might be cheating. Cheating in its many forms is to be avoided at all costs. For instance, you cannot withhold vital information from the reader if that information is known to the main character, nor can you have a revelation that is wildly improbable or inconsistent with what's already happened. It could be argued that Agatha Christie—and most whodunit writers—cheats; Scott Turow's *Presumed Innocent* is a cheat, since the book is written in the first person, yet the central poser—did the narrator commit the murder or not—is presented as a genuine conundrum. So no tricks. And where possible, revelations should come from the characters' own mouths in a way that flows naturally and logically from the story. Remember, too, that people do not normally speak in paragraphs, so keep your dialogue sharp and reasonably succinct.

Advancing the action

Dialogue can serve to advance the action in an unexpected direction, like a plot point in a film. It can in fact be advantageous when writing a crime scene to see it as a scene in a film, even to the extent of visualising characters as well-known actors. The hitman Alfie Meehan, from *Catspaw*, looks like Bruno Lawrence, while Don Bartholomew bears a striking resemblance to Bryan Brown. Dennis Gatz looks something like Colin Friels, and so on. As well as helping you flesh out your characters, this device gives them their voice, thereby making the dialogue easier to write.

Here's a passage from *Stingray* in which two senior homicide cops, Chris and Kerry, try to work out what to do about the fact that a young colleague, Shane, has just killed his wife in a fit of jealous rage. This is all happening in the middle of the night. The issue is complicated by a number of factors, the result of which is that Chris and Kerry find themselves having to make the toughest decision of their lives.

'What are you thinking, Chris?' Kerry said. He could feel the minutes and seconds slipping by, and had become nervous about the way this conversation was shaping up.

Chris said, 'I guess I'm thinking, so far we're the only ones that know about this, that maybe no one else needs to. But I can't believe I'm having those thoughts.'

'Shit, Chris.'

'Yeah, you said it.' He looked keenly at Kerry, saying, 'We can pull this off, mate.'

'Can we?' But pull what off, exactly?

'I think so. Are you solid?'

Kerry wasn't yet. 'I guess so.'

'That's not good enough, mate. Are you solid?' He grasped Kerry's arm. Kerry looked down at Chris's hand on his arm, then met his old partner's unwavering eyes again.

'I'm solid, Chris. I just hope you know what you're doing.'

'I told you it'll be all right. Let's go back in.'

Shane was sitting at the edge of his seat with his big killer's hands grasping his knees. The cold sweat on his face glimmered in the lamplight. He did not look like an Iron Man at all.

Chris said, 'Go and get a blanket, Shane. Then grab a rag and wipe your prints off everywhere you've been. Move it. We're outta here.'

Shane stared at him, then at Kerry. Then he got up and went to the bedroom.

It is much more interesting to advance the action in this way rather than simply stating that Kerry and Chris decided to dispose of the body. With these words the story, which began as a straight investigation, suddenly finds itself heading down a different, darker road. A single conversation can turn everything around in a minute.

Tags: He said, she said

A word on tags. For such a minor and basic element in fiction writing, they cause a lot of headaches. The thing to realise is that tags should not be intrusive. In fact they should not be noticed at all. Eschew elaborate ones that attract the reader's eye, like 'retorted', 'declared', 'inquired', 'riposted' and so on. Remember that the old mainstay 'said' is invisible. Often a passage of dialogue can manage perfectly well without tags, except if the conversation goes on for a while. In a long piece of dialogue a tag line can be used to give the character (and the reader) room to breathe, e.g. 'And that's only the beginning,' he said, reaching for his beer. 'When I got there the place had been trashed. The bathroom mirror was smashed, white powder everywhere, pizza stuck to the walls.' Adverbs are like hand grenades, to be used sparingly and with great care. If you wish to give the impression that a person is speaking angrily, uncertainly or whatever, show it through behaviour rather than by using an adverb.

EXERCISE

1. Switch on the TV and turn the sound down. This is an exercise not in guessing what the characters are actually saying but in making use of the gestures and attitudes of the speakers to trigger your imagination. Imagine a scenario. Use dialogue to give the reader an idea of what's happening, and the relationship between the characters.

    or

    Choose a real-life restaurant, park, anywhere you can see people talking but not hear them. They are probably talking about the weather, but this is the world of crime and everyone is a suspect. Are they two undercover cops? Is the waiter explaining the menu passing on coded information? What are they *really* saying?

7 BEGINNINGS, ENDINGS AND BITS IN BETWEEN

Robert Wallace

Beginnings: Starting with a bang or a whimper?

There are as many jokes sporting that da-da-da-dum start to Beethoven's Fifth Piano Concerto as their gag line as there are musical farces playing games with splutteringly pompous symphonic endings. These musical conventions for starting and finishing can so easily be made to appear absurd, yet they are important because they emphasise the separateness of a piece of music from the continuum of time and space. A composition has to start somewhere, even if to start, and thereby command attention, is in itself absurd. The writer of any work of fiction is faced with the question: How should I begin? For the writer of crime fiction the question is particularly important.

I started *Paint Out* with: 'I was thrown by the force of the explosion.' I started *To Catch a Forger*:

> There was nothing much in the room: a bed, a stack of
> dusty paintings against the wall. A blanket was folded on the
> stained mattress. In the kitchen: a fork, a spoon, a plate. No

saucepans. The potted geraniums had gone from a balcony just wide enough to hold them.

The telephone rang.

'Essington?'

Sometimes I wish convention would allow for the reader to be eased into a story, that the gap between consciousness outside of reading a book and that within the book could be bridged so the reader sort of drifted into a narrative instead of being hit over the head; instead of the start saying to the reader, 'Hey, something's happening, pay attention.'

These days publishers' editors want a book to bite on page 1 and hang on like a pit bull terrier for at least the first third of its length. After that I guess they don't care so much, as long as there is an effective ending. The thinking behind this attitude is that once a reader has travelled through the first third, they are almost certain to read to the end, to find out where all this is going. The most corny device used to grab the reader is to excise a particularly chilling part of the narrative and hang it, out of sequence, as a prologue—like a carrot dangling in front of a donkey. You read that bit of sensational action and then plough on to discover how it came to pass that, say, three blood-smeared werewolves/merchant bankers were slicing up a boy scout with an electric carving knife.

The need for this kind of sensational reader-grabbing device arises, I suspect, from a consciousness that TV-age distraction seekers easily become bored. There are many more things to do than read.

However, while aware of their audience, most crime writers wish to avoid becoming abject slaves of the market. They have dignity. They want to sustain at least the illusion of creative integrity. So, there is a tension between, on the one hand, the creative need to break rules with experimental openings and, on the other hand, the reality of the general reader's expectations.

I started *An Axe to Grind*: 'Apparently, like Trotsky, the old lady took a lot of killing.' Very conventional. In *Food Rain* I used a prologue, not to hang a sensational scene out the front, but rather to introduce a nature theme:

> What was that? A scream, perhaps? An agonised human cry breaking the pre-dawn quiet, beating the birds to their day? Or is it that you can never know the meaning of a sound once the moment has passed? Because in the end nature swallows everything.

The opening pages

I am someone who starts writing at the beginning and ends at the end, making it up as I go along. Most of my work, after I have completed the first draft, consists of reworking the opening ten pages, struggling to get them into a satisfying relationship with all that comes after. In my initial draft the first pages are no more than evidence of my blind search for a story. They may be building a sense of place, or sketching in a character, but they will always be vague and ill formed.

Elmore Leonard says he might establish a character in the first twenty pages only to lose interest and transfer attention to someone new who happens to saunter into the narrative.

Most writers I know work out a general structure before starting the first chapter, or, having such a plan, decide to start somewhere other than at the beginning. I have heard of authors (before the personal computer) writing notes on index cards, and creating a novel by building out from and around these notes and arranging and rearranging their sequence.

It doesn't matter how you attack a story, in the end you are faced with pages. The first page is No. 1. You have to hook the reader right there. Nobody knows for sure what will work—if they did writing would be more formularised than it is.

A 1950s-style start:

> A breeze off the Pacific was lifting the curtains and spreading the perfume of frangipani through my apartment. A record was stuck on the radiogram, Red Sails in the Sunset, Jo Stafford: 'Carry my loved one home safely to me.'

> A two-thirds-gone bottle of Beefeater gin was on the glass-top table, two glasses, an ashtray with three butts . . . lipstick traces.
>
> Camilla was in the bathroom. She was naked. Her perfect breasts were spread like silk either side of a bullet hole the size of a piece of confetti, or of that sapphire in the ring she wore on her right hand.

This might not work today. Or maybe you could make it work by giving it a postmodern twist. But then, next year, the postmodern slant might turn readers off. The bait on your hook has to be what people are feeding on at the time. Choosing it is always a gamble, a mystery.

Varying a formula is exciting but, to play safe, it's as well to stick in the result of a crime at the start: a corpse, say. In the classical formulation of plot, what is there at the beginning ought to be there, utterly changed, at the end. Between the start and the finish of a crime book a transformation of meanings takes place. This is what drags the reader along. They have taken the bait because the subject interests them. Now they expect to be led to some unexpected re-reading of the attendant facts. And, at the same time, they want the characters to develop. You cannot present a sequence of gradually redefined realities if, while doing so, you keep the characters immutable as statues.

On the first page of *Art Rat* I introduce the central character, the psychotic killer-artist Glyn. He is lying in the bath:

> Head wreathed in steam, Glyn was soaking himself, topping up by turning the hot water tap on with his foot. He thought about the red-haired woman who had spent that night under the same roof, thought about Roy Summers groping over the surface of her body.

At the end of the book, Lupo, who is Glyn reborn as a media-packaged artist, dies wading through deep snow. Readers might not have registered it, but I got some satisfaction out of the central character starting in steaming bath water, ending in snow. For me, those two moments placed what came between in a context. The water motif is repeated throughout the narrative, connecting elements of the story. If such a device is obvious it can seem sophomoric, cornball. You don't need to try hard for that sort of thing because the mind will unconsciously produce linkages like the water theme anyway.

Most of the best of what writers do is uncontrived: they hardly know they have done it till they arrive at the editing stage. The worst that writers produce arises out of conscious intellectual striving.

In even the most stilted of 1930s British country-house murder mysteries—'cosies'—it was *de rigueur* for the killer to be introduced, but not identified, by the end of the first chapter. Thus the killer appeared pretty soon after, or even before, Lord So and So was found in the duck pond, a silly grin on his face, a piano-wire garotte tight around his neck. The first chapter introduced the reader to a ritualised game involving working out which of the cast of upper-class twits did Lord So and So in. In such a book the chapters in the middle, that is between the first chapter and the last, were intended to tease the reader's expectations and allow the writer space in which to present to the audience a number of character sketches. As well, of course, it was in the material of these chapters that clues and red herrings were embedded.

The start of a book sets an atmosphere, it functions as a trigger for the reader's imagination. Once this is activated, unless there's a very good reason for doing otherwise, the reader should stick with you. So the start, whether it contains a crime scene or whether it eases towards the criminal act, should provide a kind of imaginative space into which the reader shifts.

PI books tend to establish the imaginative space and set the action rolling by having the client make contact with the investigator. They sketch in as the scene a grim office the rent of which is in arrears. Life is hard. The PI is desperate for a job. The phone rings or, these days, a message spews out of the fax machine. In a standard PI book, several of the problems of introducing a story are overcome by convention. This is not to say that the PI book is easier to write than books in other subgenres; having a convention with which to start is useful, but later on the PI writer must battle with the problem of repetition.

PI book or not, if at the start the phone rings it has to be good because so many phones have rung in so many books. Maybe, and I seem to remember this from Chandler, the phone rings and is answered while the real plot walks through the door. If it's true that what's there at the start of a book ought to be there at the end, then having someone come through the door while the phone is being answered has the great advantage of bringing three characters to the reader's attention in one paragraph. If the characters are to stay in the reader's attention, they must be memorable. They need to go part of the way towards establishing the atmosphere of the book. If you intend to concentrate on one-liners, maybe this is the time to bring one in. If the tone is to be unrelentingly grim, realistic, mean, this is the time to set it. You can do this with description but, better still, you can do it by allowing the characters to speak for themselves and act out the atmosphere.

Without a PI or professional investigative presence of some sort at the start, you will have to find some other way to tell the reader why the book exists (more of that later), but you will also enjoy a certain freedom at the start.

You may, if you like, begin with a detailed description of a crime being committed, but if your main character is a PI this raises the question of point of view: Who knows and observes these things? If it is the PI, then there may be no need for an investigation.

If you choose to start at the crime scene, while the crime is being committed, then you may have your characters attempt to catch up with knowledge that you, as writer, and your readers already possess.

You may choose to begin with a psychological case study. Or perhaps the central character—this would produce a book in the paranoia mould—is caught, red handed, at the scene of a crime. Only he didn't do it. But nobody believes him.

A psychological case study can produce an electric charge right at the start of a book, building in the reader a whole pattern of expectations which may or may not later be fulfilled. If, for instance, from the first sentence you step inside the head of a real crazy, bowling through a shopping mall, in her imagination going kaboom, kaboom, blowing up everything she sees, producing everybody's nightmare of mayhem in a crowded public place, you'll have caught the reader's attention. Then, maybe, you could devote the rest of the book to making the reader love this character and learn that the real criminal is the nice trauma counsellor character who, on seeing the crazy in the mall, rings the police but delays the evacuation of the mall until after the real bomb, which he planted to kill his paramour, goes off in a French patisserie directly opposite the toy shop.

The bits in between: A sprinkling of clues, twists, red herrings, teases

The stuff coming between start and finish should contain enough elements neatly connected with the development of plot to keep the reader going. Yet it is also in the middle that you may get away with a little self-indulgence. If, for instance, dressage is an obsession of yours—and they say you should always write about what you know—then you might offer the reader a second level of satisfaction by detailing its complexities: saddles, horse clipping, boots, jackets, bitchy remarks about bums and horses. This way, the reader will be reading on not only because he was hooked in the first chapter and wants to know the outcome of criminal intentions but also because he is getting information about an interesting aspect of the world. But however much detail you include—on photography, gardening, or breeding budgerigars—you must move the plot along briskly enough to keep the reader's attention, yet release your clues as gradually and as inconspicuously as possible. For a reader the one thing worse than being lectured to is having clues clumsily underscored. Readers do not want their IQs questioned.

If you happen to be writing a police procedural, then the discovery of evidence and its interpretation will be fairly easy to handle because you are simply writing an account of how such things are routinely processed. Thus, people in white coats arrive at the scene of the crime while the principal character—a detective, say—wrestles with the desire to smoke. A little later on, in the interest of providing the reader with information about the world, the detective may start a course of hypnotherapy to help him kick the habit—just before visiting a forensic scientist who discusses with him the significance of fibres, stains and cartridges discovered at the scene of the crime. It is perfectly natural in procedurals for characters to spell out to each other which pieces of evidence signify what.

But where a novel's central character is a citizen who has been caught up in something, the clues are more difficult to handle. Dashiell Hammett's Sam Spade, for instance, even though he's a PI with tenuous police connections, seems to spend most of his time wandering and wondering, getting the hots for shady ladies and being clobbered over the head. Sam is representative of us little people, bamboozled by a world too corrupt and unpredictable to comprehend. Clues in Hammett-esque stories are less logically driven than in a procedural; the PI is concussed too often to follow the plot. His being life's fall guy is the point of the story. In such books, and there are many—Peter Corris's Cliff Hardy stories are an example—the principal plot interest does not reside in the clues, nor indeed in the solution to the crime. These books are about cities—Sydney, Munich, Los Angeles—and about postmodern, essentially existentialist heroes—or anti-heroes—with whom the reader travels along life's mean streets.

Major plot twists, shifts in how things look investigation-wise, should be positioned with care. You will notice in mass-market films that the slant of the plot shifts somewhere around a third of the way through. This is true also of books. Thus, in the case of a hypothetical British country-house 'cosy', one-third of the way through the scene shifts to London, or some hitherto minor character comes barging into the action's centre. Or a second corpse throws the investigation wide open again.

Similarly, one-third from the end, a writer might introduce an abrupt change of atmosphere—suddenly, danger from an unexpected quarter stalks the main character.

Normally you will have at least two formal plot devices running at the same time. The first might involve the notion that what is in the first chapter must be in the last—otherwise purists will regard you as a cheat. I wouldn't insist on this but I would worry if, having bothered with characters, places, details along the way, in the end you have the criminal turn out to be, say, a previously unhinted-at creature from outer space. Sure, Lord So and So may be killed by a creature from outer space if, in the first chapter, the amphetamine-addicted maid remembers seeing 'a strange light and something kind of like a big cigar. It was sort of floating just above the lawn, governor.' But if there has been no hint that creatures from outer space may be involved, introducing one at the end is liable to give the game away: readers will realise that you have lost the plot. A second formal device may involve sharp plot changes one-third and two-thirds of the way through.

In the interests of holding your story together, you may herald clues before clearly presenting them to the reader. Thus, a plastic shopping bag carried by a woman observed catching a bus in Sydney's Oxford Street appears as a fleeting glimpse of the bag's pattern or logo, which will register in the reader's mind as no more than a small detail of the busy street scene. You may have the traffic gridlocked so the central character, who is walking, catches up with the bus he's missed two stops before. First the shopping bag, then a nattily dressed elderly gentleman carrying it, emerge through the rear doors. Then come more details of the traffic snarl, heat building up in the late afternoon, clouds massing in the south, a sex shop's window display. The bag is momentarily unattended at the bus stop, no elderly man in sight. Look away, look back, the bag is gone. Now your bag is embedded in the plot. There's no need to mention it again until it's needed.

Such scattering of clues, use of detail, teasing of the reader's mind—catch-me-if-you-can fiction—may be manipulated to create a kind of anxiety in the reader. If your plot is tending towards the thriller end of the genre, one of the devices at your disposal is failure to satisfy the reader's desire to 'see' anticipated horrors. As with on-screen sex, described horrors are rather less disturbing—or titillating—than those left as dimensionless hopes or fears. The teasing of reader expectations, by lingering over the detail of placing a bet on the TAB, say, when the reader is anticipating some terrible revelation or act of savagery, is a useful ploy.

The best model for teasing the reader, to my mind, is Henry James. In his *The Princess Cassimassima*, you know that something terrible is going to happen, you page-turn to the final 5000 words, and still he prattles on about small things, life's details, in the most infuriating fashion. The action you have been speeding so slowly towards takes place in the book's last paragraph.

Having a narrating 'I' from whose point of view you tell the story enables you to slip in semi-apprehended clues as part of the narrator's thought process. The limitation of this first-person point of view is, of course, that the reader can only know what the narrator can know. If the 'I' is answering the phone, he cannot know that the caller is looking out the window at a killing and saying nothing about it. The third-person point of view, on the other hand, usually assumes that, like God, you as author are omnipresent and virtually omniscient. The reader may become irritated if he catches you withholding information. Recently the differing limitations of first and third-person narratives have been overcome by writers breaking the rules, changing from first to third person, chapter by chapter, shifting from past to present tense, to enable more evidence to be presented.

Then there are red herrings. Guns, say. Caching guns may keep the reader on edge. A character comes home, puts a handgun on the kitchen table. Her house-husband objects, saying that a .38 automatic is the last thing the kids need, particularly Wayne, who is a trouble maker at school. When this develops into a conversation about the role of parents, the house-husband hides the gun on the top shelf of the bathroom cabinet. As the story unfolds this gun may be relocated several times but never brought into play. Handled in the right manner, a device such as this may sustain an absurdist subplot while the real heart of the story develops.

Where there is no investigator, the writer's task is more complicated. The reader will ask: Why is this person involved? Why not take this situation to the police? In a plot of this type, the presentation and interpretation of clues throughout the narrative become problematic. There is, of course no opportunity for the main character to deal with forensic evidence or research people's backgrounds.

There are means of placing the reader on the inside and the main character on the outside so the reader, as if from on high, becomes engaged in the character's confusion: A dripping umbrella is in the hallway of a rooming house. Then it's removed. Your hero comes upon a pool of water where the umbrella has been but he can't work out how the water got there. The reader knows, he doesn't.

Endings: Surprise? Surprise!

Endings are superficially the easiest but actually the most difficult part of writing in the crime genre. Often, as a reader, I sail through the first two-thirds of a book, happy as a tortoise, and then, coming into the straight, I sense the strain on the author. The worst kinds of endings are those that introduce outside elements—characters from outer space—for the sole purpose of digging the author out of a hole. But there are a number of other pitfalls. In the final third the author may start jerking too hard on the strings operating the story's puppets. Doing this can erase subtleties of character hinted at earlier on. Perhaps the transition from creepy-guy-around-the-district to angry killer is depicted as too total. Yes, I guess the greatest danger with endings is that characters who previously were well rounded may become cardboard cutouts. Of course, if the book is anti-naturalistic, this may not present a problem, because the reader will have adjusted to an arbitrary representation of people and places.

There is always the kind of ending where several characters are placed in a cliché nightmare situation—on top of a cliff, in a cave, in a boat in the middle of a lake, on top of a 50-storey building. Such endings often fail to connect with what has come before unless—and I have seen this done well—they pinpoint the book's penultimate moment; then, after the reader has been dragged screaming to almost certain death, the real conclusion creeps up with stealth.

Another problematic type of ending, returning to the country-house 'cosy' model, is where characters stand about in the drawing room while the detective interprets the clues out loud. The butler fills tea cups, the younger son fidgets, Mummy takes poison. All that has come before may have been convincing, engaging, but this kind of stylised conclusion has to be written with great skill to avoid falling flat.

Variations on the country-house/clue-puzzle conclusion all involve explanation of what has come before. With thinly veiled condescension, the detective explains to those weekend guests still alive—and to the reader—what anybody ought to have been able to work out for themselves: Why there was a dog hair on the carpet; why the leg of the chair was on the cuff of a corpse's trousers; what it means for a Waterford crystal decanter to be tipped over without the wine spilling; at what hour a goldfish is normally fed. With this kind of ending, you risk writing down to your readers or, worse still, spelling out what was not properly articulated earlier in the book.

I admit to disliking explanatory endings, whether they involve a detective or just a mix of characters.

> 'When you claimed you thought Margery was in the boatshed varnishing that dinghy, she was actually in Perth completing an options play involving Indian Ocean Television, which gave me control of Wilfax, which owns 47 per cent of Indian Ocean.'
>
> 'She couldn't have been, Stella, because on the day of the Indian Ocean trade she was with Brendan, practising salsa at Gina's dancing school.'
>
> 'I've got to tell you, Nancy, when Margery first landed in Brisbane, she didn't intend to stay. Her family paid to get her out of New York because her father was running for district attorney and . . .'
>
> 'You're not saying that Margery was . . .'

'Of course I am, sweetie. Margery was pregnant when she hit Brisbane.'

'I don't get it, why Brisbane? Why would an east coast lawyer send his pregnant daughter to Brisbane?'

'Brendan wasn't her father.'

'Not her father!'

'No . . . and when the twins were born . . .'

'Wayne and Brett are twins, and Margery's their . . .!'

'Two boys.'

'How can you be so sure?'

'Margery and I, before my sex-change operation, we were brother and sister.'

'Were?' But when she was working on the dinghy . . .'

'Forget about the boatshed. I'm sorry, Nancy, Margery fell under the Indian Pacific outside Kalgoorlie.'

'Fell?'

'That's the way the police are reading it.' Stella watched the strain go out of Nancy's face. She ordered another caffè latte, asked if Nancy wanted the same. But Nancy was already on her feet. At the door of the cafe she turned. 'And how do you read it, Stella, or should I say, Warner?' she asked.

'It's no use, Nancy, I already rang Sergeant Barker, he knows about you and the Satellite Dinghy Syndicate.'

'You've been playing with me, haven't you, and I thought you were my . . .' Nancy had a blowpipe in her hand, she was bringing it to her bee-stung lips. Stella froze.

Deftly, the coffee jockey removed her Donald Duck mask. It was Margery, in her hand a chrome-plated Saturday-night special. She stepped from behind the espresso machine. 'Give me that blowpipe,' she said. 'As you see, Nance, I didn't catch no train.'

Nancy screamed like a chimpanzee on heat, and, fainting, got herself in the foot with the poison dart.

To pull off a surprise ending you must have embedded some antecedents in the plot, otherwise it's going to read like a last-ditch invention by a desperate author. The surprise ending requires a deft touch earlier in the narrative, as the pieces of evidence that make it possible must be sprinkled like fairy dust across the action. When you are writing in the first person, your surprise ending must be capable of surprising your narrator. This presents a problem because the intelligent reader may work back over the book and ask, How can the narrator not have noticed this? Or that?

Particular problems are posed by exceptionally tricksy plots, where, for instance, the reader discovers at the end that the first-person narrator is actually the perpetrator of the crime. How can you effect this? Well the first-person narrator may have amnesia. Or your storyline may be constructed in such a way that the narrator is describing one set of events while only dropping hints as to the causes of a second set that at some point transmute into the main plot. Let us suppose, for example, that a PI is asked by his sister, a wealthy widow, to search for her daughter. This sister treats him with contempt because she's somebody and he's a failure. He is getting nowhere with the investigation when his sister dies in an accident, news of which is introduced to the reader via a fax the PI receives. The PI continues tracing the missing daughter, eventually finding her in an ashram in Queensland. He explains that her mother is dead. Beyond worldly concerns, the daughter has cancer, has days to live, is not interested. The PI returns to base, presents the mother's will to the lawyers, inherits everything. And that's the penultimate moment in the book. In the next chapter, the investigator is having fun running his hotel on the Great Barrier Reef. A bunch of religious freaks come by one morning. They wear robes, have shaved heads, look bad. Our PI tells them to shove off, they are scaring the customers, they are upsetting his pair of pedigree corgis.

With one page to go, this is the moment when a surprise ending might work. An unwashed, lecherous, fat guru, with hippie bimbo in tow, turns up at the motel three weeks later, demanding money. He accuses the PI of killing his dead follower's mother. The PI calls in the police. The guru is removed. The cult is discredited in the press. And then—last paragraph—it is time to produce the one piece of evidence embedded in the plot that fingers the PI. Our Mr Good-guy PI rigged the accident that killed his sister. If she hadn't been dying of cancer he would have killed the daughter as well. End of story.

Exercises

Beginnings
1. Look at story openings that really grabbed you. Analyse them to work out how this effect is produced.

2. Take the first sentence of a book as a starter and continue to write your version of the opening page.

3. Write three opening sentences of your own, choose the one that most appeals and continue with the opening paragraph.

4. Choose a movie that has a gripping opening scene. Write this scene as the opening of a novel.

Endings
1. Read the first chapter (or until you get to the incident that sets the story going) of a new book by one of your favourite crime writers. Now write your own conclusion.

8 SETTING, ACTION AND SUSPENSE

Nigel Krauth

11.05 a.m. The phone rang. It was long distance. The beeps didn't help my hangover.

'It's Marele Day,' the voice said.

I mentally flicked through my Refedex. 'Not *the* Marele Day,' I croaked.

'That's the one,' she said. 'I want to employ you. I want you to do an investigation for me.'

'I'm in the investigations business,' I said. 'What's the problem?'

There was a moment's silence. Maybe she was reaching for a cigarette. Then she said, 'I want you to write about Setting, Action and Suspense.'

I didn't ask her to repeat it. I had heard right. I reached for a cigarette of my own.

'That's a tough assignment,' I said. 'I'm expensive.'

'Hang the cost, Mr Krauth. All I want is a result. You know what I mean?'

I liked the toughness in her voice. I like tough dames. And I liked the assignment too. Setting, Action and Suspense. An investigation I could get my teeth into. I lit the cigarette.

'What's the fee?' I asked.

'We'll talk about that later. When can you get started?'

She didn't mince words. It was a good sign.

'I'm pretty busy right now,' I lied. 'But I'll find a space. I could do the preliminaries straight away.'

'That's fine. Keep in touch.'

She rang off. I finished the cigarette, spilling ash over my keyboard. I blew it away and shoved in a battered floppy. I booted up the old Deltacom. It blinked and beeped at me. 'Enter your codename,' it said. 'Enter your password.'

There are codenames and passwords in the genre of crime writing. You need to know them. You need to know them so you can use them and break them. All writing is investigation. Investigators obey the rules until they become desperate. There is nothing more desperate than a desperate writer. All writing is knowing the rules and breaking them.

I sat and had another think about the phone call. What the hell. It was 11.18. I had a bottle of Jean-Pierre champagne in the office fridge. Why not pop it? Setting, Action and Suspense, I thought. It sounded like a firm of lawyers. You've got to go about this one in a systematic manner, I told myself. Setting. Action. Suspense. Three different leads. Three different locales. Three different negotiating points in the writing process. What was the link?

I decided to break them up. Investigate them separately. Then think about the connections. There's nothing unrelated in this postmodern world. That's an overall fact.

Setting

I always start with setting. I do this because the crime genre always starts with setting. You can set a crime novel in San Francisco, Miami, or New York. If you're game you can set it in Richmond, Virginia. In Australia you can set a crime novel in Sydney or in Surfers Paradise, but you can't set it in Melbourne. Melbourne is the setting for spy novels. That sounds like a rule. Rules were meant to be broken.

The settings for crime novels must have glamour. You know what I mean? The settings must be places which give a twinge between the thighs. It's a sexual thing. It's about thrills. Crime is about thrills. Those other guys, the readers, are reading this stuff for thrills. There are thrilling places, thrilling times. Investigate them. Sydney in the 1930s. San Francisco in the '50s and '60s. Miami in the '70s and '80s. Hollywood any time since the '20s. Surfers now.

Why's this a fact? Perhaps it's because the crime novel is linked to something deep in our psychologies, something about our cultural hopes. Something about our ideals. Our misplaced ideals. Who knows? Who knows the mind of the murderer, the serial killer, the rapist? The corrupt cop, the paid assassin, the snuff-movie maker? Who knows the mind of the culture?

I don't know. I'm just an investigator. I search inside for the answers.

The ultimate setting of the crime thriller is the human heart. Sounds corny, but it's true. The human heart is a fickle place. For a time the Australian human heart was stranded in the English countryside. We got over that. We toyed with Europe (while Simenon and Charteris were writing) and with San Francisco (while Carter Brown misread the road directory). Nowadays the Australian human heart sites itself in various American locales, or those Australian locales which appeal in an American way. Crime is about cultural aspirations, as I said. Investigate the culture and you'll find the clues to where the heart is placed. The heart is the CBD of crime. Watch the six o'clock news. It's a dead giveaway.

The key point here is that settings for crime fiction must be exotic and exciting. Or, if you want to break the mould, you've got to prove the exoticness and excitingness of your chosen place and time. Or (and there is always a solution you didn't think of) you can choose anywhere, anytime (say, Melbourne, circa 1885) and make it work by knowing it intimately. Fascinating crime can happen anytime, anywhere. It's a matter of finding the drama and tensions in a landscape or an architecture or an era. Don't set your crime story in a boring place or time. Make it tense and exciting, no matter how boring it really is. But, then again, are there any boring places or times?

I got that far in my thinking, then the champagne took over. I was three bottles down the track, admittedly, but I never drive when I drink. I just write. Or phone up. They'll probably bring in a law against drink-phoning. Too bad. At the moment it's still legal.

'Marele?'

'Yes?'

'Sorry to bother you, pal. I've had a breakthrough. I'm saying that all writing is investigation. You know what I mean? And it's especially so with setting. Everyone thinks that setting is just description. But what do they work on down at the CIB, eh? Descriptions. What is a PI's stuff in trade? Descriptions. What does the judge want, eh? Descriptions. Investigation is about description. Therefore all writing is about description. You describe setting, action, suspense, character, plot, talk, thoughts, themes, and all the links between. You describe them. See what I mean?'

'I'm surprised, Mr Krauth. Did you ring me just to tell me this?'

'Sorry, Marele. You did say to keep in touch.'

'Keep in touch. Yes. And keep in control.'

'Okay, Marele. Nice talking to you.'

I put the phone down, and pulled out another Jean-Pierre. So that you'll know—so that you can see it—I'll admit I only drink the pink. The Rose, they call it. By any other name it would taste the same. And have the same effect. Nice thing about cheap champagne, though, you don't need a bottle-opener. Just strong hands. And a tough brain and heart. The same with crime writing.

Investigate your settings. Setting will tell you almost everything. Setting will tell you the mood, the possibilities and limits of the action, the shape of the plot, the nature of the characters. Put your settings into an identification line-up. Photograph them from the front and from the side. Arrange a stake-out. Certain crimes happen in certain settings. A hotel corridor, a steel mill locker room, the deck of a businessman's yacht, a maternity ward, an old people's home, a church vestry, a police station, a university staff room, a urinal in the park, a deserted beach, a sex shop, your own kitchen. They each have their particular potential crime. And that means their particular characters, action, and mood. And often the locations provide you (eventually) with all the other elements of your fiction— the issues, the emotions, the drama, the language texture.

Setting is a stool pigeon. Setting will give you the first lead. Setting will set you up in crime writing. And the great thing about setting is: it's already there. All you have to do is describe it. But your description has to be good. Researched, sharp, and detailed. And sexy, as I said. No fugitive (especially a piece of crime fiction) ever escaped when there was a good description current.

And getting back to that other thing about setting: don't forget the heart bit. All crimes are set in the heart before they find their external settings. Interrogate yourself. Where would you kill your mother, your boyfriend, your psychiatrist, your local constable? All in the same place? Well, yes, you'd kill them in your heart first, and then you'd find a special place elsewhere in the world for each of them.

'Marele?'

'Don't tell me . . .'

'Yes. It's me again. I think I've got a pretty good description of setting for you. I've nailed it down. I think we're looking at a result here. I know it's early times but . . .'

'It's twenty past eleven, Mr Krauth. It says so on my bedside clock. That's way too late for me. Why don't you ring me again in the morning? Late in the morning, I mean.'

'I'm sorry, Marele. I'm a man of action. You know what I'm saying? When I want to do it, I've got to do it.'

'Do it on your own, buster. I'm putting this phone off the hook right now . . .'

She was tough all right. I liked that. I don't have any problem with tough women. They're exciting. Tough women are more interesting than tough men. I don't know why. It must be a cultural thing. There's nothing that isn't a cultural thing these days.

The heart of the culture. That's something to cut out and examine.

If I say murder in a public urinal, you think gays or pederasts, don't you? If I say murder in your own kitchen, you think domestic. If I say deserted beach, you think no relation between murderer and victim. Thrill kill. Rape and the fishing knife going in. If I say murder in a meatworks, an art gallery, a police station, you don't think any of the above.

Setting has meanings, makes statements. Setting has its stereotypes, its archetypes. Use them, or avoid them. Change the setting and you change everything else. Setting can reinforce central themes, character constructions, plot and action. Or it can contrast with them. I call that one ironic setting. A domestic murder in a public urinal? Why not? Go against the stereotype. The father did it. He hated the idea of his son turning out gay. Bizarre stuff. The culture is the culprit. Nail it.

Setting isn't just background, local colour, atmosphere, texture. Setting is metaphor, symbol, imagery. Setting says things. It's more than description. It's analysis. Of themes, character, plot meanings. Setting works on several levels. It generates ideas. The details of setting give the game away. Ask any good investigator. What did you see at the scene of the crime? I saw the whole thing happen, in retrospect.

'Sweetheart?'

'Who is this?'

'Who do you think?'

'*Jesus Christ!*'

'No, not him.'

'Don't you ever sleep, Mr Krauth?'

'Not if I can help it.'

'It's 3.07.'

'Yeah, I know. The bedside clock. This is costing me, Marele. I've been through six bottles of Jean-Pierre. I work to a budget, you know. At a bottle a page, things get expensive. I think we should talk about the fee.'

'Not at 3.08 in the morning. I'm not in the mood for it. I'm putting this phone off the hook right now . . .'

'You said that the last time, Marele . . . Marele?'

Action

At this point I decided to watch a movie. There's a 24-hour video store down on the corner. They have all their movies on marked shelves. Comedy, Drama, Action, R-Rated. At 3.13 a.m. you can pick and choose from the R-Rated shelf without anyone bothering you much. So I didn't bother the pale-looking guy in stubby shorts at the R-Rated shelf, I went straight to the Action section. I looked for something useful. There were 27 copies of *Delta Force*, and none of *Duel*. I picked up *Tequila Sunrise*, *Bonnie and Clyde* and *The Untouchables*, and headed for the cashier.

If you want to know about action you should investigate films and actors. Action is a visual business, no matter whether you're narrating in the first, second or third person. But action's also a feeling business. Others see the action you do (and the doer sees it too). At the same time, you feel the action you do (and sometimes the other feels it too, of course).

So when you're writing about action you've got to see it from various angles and feel it from various angles. Especially if you're using an anonymous-narrator, multiple-character point of view. You know what I mean? Really see it. Really feel it. You've got to get right into it. Get right inside it. And allow it to get right inside you. You've got to run it through your head like a movie to get the pace right, get the continuity right, get the emphases and the balances right. Actually, you've got to run it on your mind's screen in slow motion, to get the real beauty or horror of it. The musculature. The aesthetics.

If the girl in your story has to move off the bed, find the gun in her purse and aim it at the guy who's been screwing her, then you have a lot of camera angles to consider, a lot of limb and body movements to keep in (or out of) frame, a lot of shapes and outlines and shadows and substantialities to make decisions about. You have to look at it frame by single frame—analyse it, weigh it. And you have to look at each sequence of actions in total, as a fluid movement, a transformation through space and time, a dance. There are 114 muscles involved in just smiling at someone, imagine how many muscles are involved in killing someone. And there are a million perspectives on any one bit of action. The perspective of the doer. The perspective of the done to. And the perspective of the 999,998 flies on the wall.

Narrative viewpoint can't be ignored here: the question of the distance between the view source and the action. Where is the camera situated? In the head of the doer? In the head of the done to? In the head of the fly on the wall? Study each frame. The action is different if the girl holds the camera at the same time as she holds the gun, or if the guy holds the camera at the same time as he holds his dick, or if the fly is sitting on the surveillance equipment lens. There's no *right* viewpoint to take, but it does depend on viewpoint decisions you make overall.

In addition to the way action looks, there's the way action feels. Don't write anything unless you're sure you know how it feels. To punch. To kiss. To slip a knife into a fat constable. To rape an eight-year-old. Do it in your head, and in your body. Go through the motions. Analyse them. Do it in slow motion. Use the jog and shuttle. Know what it feels like intimately. Let your body feel the doing of it to someone. Let your body feel it done to you. Know it, then write it. Write it so the reader knows the feeling. Every subtle, provocative, ineluctable, horrific, thrilling bit. The investigator doesn't have blood on his/her hands. Not always. But he knows what it's like. He's seen it up close too often not to know. Seen it in the head and the body and the heart, close and often enough to reproduce it in detail.

But there are other ways too. There are always other ways. There are ways of seeing without having seen, of saying without saying. Ways of suggesting. Sometimes action is best described by not describing at all. Here you rely on the reader's own knowledge, which is as good as your own. Why does your reader want to read the stuff you write? Because s/he wants thrills. The same thrills you get from writing. Readers are great writers, they just don't know it. So leave a gap and let them fill it in. Let them provide the subtlety, the provocation, the intellectuality, the horror, the thrills. Hand the camera over to the reader. 'You film this bit in your own head', you can say. 'You provide the frame-by-frame action, and the police photographer's still shot.' But give the reader the clues to the action, and the result, if you want the gap filled. The girl moves from the bed, she finds the gun in her purse . . . Blackout. Three stars, centred, on the old computer screen. A gap in the text. New section. The investigating officers find the guy with his dick in his hand, the bedclothes around him crimson, and the cassette in his camera out of tape.

'You said you'd call me late in the morning, Mr Krauth. I don't consider nine o'clock to be late.'

'Yes, Marele. I thought you'd say that. But the sun's been up for four hours. I saw it do its thing. It comes up with a jerk, you know. One minute it's not there, the next minute it is. It happens like that every day.'

'Get on with it, will you? I hate talking before breakfast.'

'We've got a problem, Marele. With the action bit. I've been following all the leads on intimate action. You know what I mean? The trajectory and mass and passage through time of a swinging fist. The subtle archings and tensions of necks and chests in a kiss. That sort of stuff. And I've done a rundown on the gap, the hiatus, the undescribed action. But it's occurred to me that I might be barking up the wrong tree. There's another action, isn't there, in a crime story? The big action. The total action. You know what I'm getting at? The whole shape of the action from the time the phone rings and there's a dame with a husky voice on the other end, to the time when she hands over the fee. I mean, when you talk about action you can be talking about single, isolated actions, or you can be talking about the whole damn lot of them put together . . .'

'So?'

'Well, do you want me to talk about the whole lot of them? That's getting onto plot isn't it? Do you want me to investigate plot?'

'Don't ask me, Mr Krauth. The investigation's entirely in your hands. That's what I'm paying you for. Goodbye.'

'Hello? Hello? Are you still there, Marele?'

The overall action. Now here's where aesthetics come in again. Aesthetics are the opposite to anaesthetics. Anaesthetics stop you feeling. That's a fact. Aesthetics really get your feeling going. You get aesthetical when something beautiful king hits you. Knocks you out. Comes up behind you and grabs you by the sensitive bits. That's what the overall action should do: seduce you, engage you, turn you to putty, make you react, satisfy you. And it should do all this for the reader too.

Now, I know you're starting to read ahead here. You can tell from the clues I'm dropping that I'm leading towards Suspense, can't you? But more of that later. (Let's not give the plot away.)

The overall action is the progress and shape and subtle weaving of your investigation. It's the record of your research and the mapping of your chase. It's not just something that happens. It's something you must think out, make plans for, consider in every detail.

I've got a nice little letterhead pad. Krauth Investigations, it says. The guy at Snap Printers on the corner worked it up for me. I write down everything I think I'm going to have to do before I go and do it. I get through a lot of these pads. Jotting, figuring, working on the weaving of my investigation. I don't just go into it blind, you know. Only an idiot would do that. And if anything bad happens to me, I always come back to my pad of notes to find out where I went wrong. Or to change my notes. The overall shaping of an investigation is not an easy business. Everything has to fall into place. But you don't know what's going to fall into place and what isn't. That doesn't mean you don't plan.

And when I look at my pad and think I see the right kind of shape developing—the kind that will take me from my desk to the bank teller's counter with cheque in hand—only then do I act.

The overall action *is* the pay cheque. It's what lets you see through the maze of incidents—the possibilities, dead ends and breakthroughs—the things that work best. And how do you know what works best? Well, read Jim Thompson, James M. Cain, Dashiell Hammett, David Goodis, Cornell Woolrich, Marc Behm, Charles Willeford, James Ellroy, Elmore Leonard, Andrew Vachss, Sue Grafton, Robert B. Parker, Patricia D. Cornwell, Peter Corris, Barry Gifford, Kinky Friedman, Marele

Day, or any other best-selling crime writer who appeals to you. Each of these guys has a personal codename—a set of personal passwords—for ways through the maze. Investigate them. Find out what they think works best. Then do your own thing.

Like I already said (when I mentioned aesthetics), the overall action must be a beautiful thing. It's the shape of the body of your story. Just as every intimate action in your story has a shape which you must track down, observe in detail, and feel, so too the overall action of your work must have a particular shape, suited to the crime. Draw an outline first. On your pad, or on the carpet in chalk, if you have to. Note all the aspects, the angles, the subtle giveaway signs. Then construct. The crime story has a living shape, it is vital and energetic. It doesn't lie dormant. No clichéd crime stories get published these days. The contemporary crime story has to get out of its old drawer in the genre morgue and step lively down new mean streets. That's what overall action is about. It's a sinewy, muscular, on-the-move, on-the-make, provocative but gorgeous thing these days. Something with tits and buns and a threat of the abominable about it. Something deliciously nasty.

'Marele?'

'I've got my make-up on. I've read the newspapers. I've even written a few pages this morning. But I'd still like to know how you got my number in the first place. It's meant to be silent. Did Telecom betray me?'

'There are ways, Marele. I know a few friends of yours.'

'Some friends. What is it this time?'

'I'm ready to investigate Suspense. But I don't like the prospects.'

'Are you saying you can't handle the assignment?'

'Not exactly. It's just that Suspense always has a good alibi. Suspense has friends in high places. You know what I mean? It's hard to nail Suspense down. Suspense is slippery. Very slippery.'

'Do you want a better fee? Is that what you're saying?'

'That might be a way of putting it, Marele. We're in the really big league here. No-one's ever pinned a rap on Suspense, as far as I know.'

'"Pinned a rap"? That's pretty old slang, Mr Krauth. That's Simmonds and Newcombe stuff.'

'I know, Marele. I like the '50s and '60s. I've done my homework. I'm an investigator, remember?'

'All right. I'll do a deal. You pin a rap on Suspense and I'll up your fee 50 per cent.'

'Is that a promise?'

'Listen, buster. I'm a fiction writer. I always tell the truth.'

Suspense

Suspense is the big guy. Suspense has never been brought to trial. So it remains a matter of trial and error, I guess. You'll need friends to bring Suspense down. Friends who'll read your manuscript and say, 'Yeah, I felt it, the suspense really builds up.' Suspense is an impact thing. You can only test impact by getting the reaction of readers. '*C'est la vie*,' as Maigret might have put it.

Suspense is not a gimmick. It's to do with the fact that in the real world you only find out anything bit by bit. No knowledge comes to you whole, packaged, complete. There is always another layer. And Suspense is not a matter of you (as writer) just being a bastard and withholding information for the fun of it. When a stool pigeon does that to me I just want to break his beak.

Suspense is a matter of the balance between giving away bits of what you know (as writer) and not giving away all of what you know, because everything is sexier that way. Suspense is perhaps the most intimate aspect of the relationship between you and your reader. Suspense involves writing with an exact knowledge of your writing's effect on the reader.

Generally speaking, though, you can give away more than you think you should. That's because you *do* know what will happen, and the reader doesn't. You don't want to mystify the reader too much. That'll disengage him/her. You want the reader to be suckered in, not alienated.

Without Suspense, you rape the plotline and action, you don't give it time for tumescence, for lubrication. Okay, rape may be your thing, but not everybody likes it. With Suspense, you start at the toes, or the fingertips. You spend time on the shoulders, the ears, the small of the back, the belly and thighs. You make the experience excruciatingly delightful. You and the reader both know you're heading for some sort of climax, but just when it'll happen, and how, is only gradually, deliciously, perhaps painfully approached. Suspense is titillation and torture, promises and threats, the ecstasy and the agony.

You'll find Suspense in a striptease joint. Suspense runs a whole string of these places. The kind of dive where the important bits are gradually revealed, or where the coverings can come off and go back on again to be revealed in a different way later. But you don't have to go to a strip show for Suspense. Suspense is in the kitchen when you're cooking a meal. (How will the can of baked beans go with the jar of caviar?) Suspense is there when you open a bottle of cheap champagne. (Will it explode, froth onto your monitor, blow the old keyboard?) Suspense is with you every minute of the day. (Will you get paid for the work you're slaving over right now?)

Suspense may be everywhere, but it's still elusive. It's hard to capture, yet it's not completely unassailable. Suspense has a track record. Suspense has given itself away in terms of red herrings, dead ends, and the stealth of introducing possibilities and suggestions. In each of these cases, when you look at a graph of the plotline, Suspense leaves its fingerprints on false crests, on giving the reader something which is satisfying for the moment, but not necessarily satisfying overall. In other words, the reader is led to believe that s/he knows what's going on, or what's likely to be going on, but things are not nailed down yet. They're still cooking. The cork is coming out tantalisingly slowly. The cheque is in the mail.

The Suspense plotline looks like this on my Snap Printers notepad:

It reminds me of the time I had to trek into the Blue Mountains National Park. I was acting on information given, looking for a body, of course, on top of a mountain, of all places. What I found, mainly, was that at each false crest I thought I had climbed the mountain, while in fact there was still a long way to go. Tantalising, agonising stuff. Psychologically, though, each false crest was wonderful. I believed I had arrived at the top of the ridge. I sat down and said, 'I've made it.' Then I looked around and saw the rest of the climb waiting. That's Suspense. Thinking you're there when you aren't. But there are dangers. The complications you introduce for the sake of Suspense mustn't interfere with the momentum of the story. You've got to think about the overall dynamics of the action. You've got to keep climbing, and pretty damn fast too.

Suspense is also a matter of setting. Atmospherics and mood. Describe the environment in an unpredictable but potent way, full of suggestion, uncertainty, expectation. Lie in bed and listen to the creaking of your house. You imagine intruders. Suspense is about how idiotic everyone's (especially your reader's) predictive imagination is. How vulnerable it is. Suspense takes the reader for a sucker. Suspense is a standover merchant. Suspense will send its goons around at midnight. Or perhaps at 4 a.m. Tomorrow maybe. Or the next day.

Suspense is also about what characters say. You know how gossip works. You know how people mis-see things, mis-know what they think they know. Talk doesn't necessarily have any basis in reality. But sometimes it does. Suspense is about knowing and not knowing. Dialogue is useful for Suspense because it leads and misleads. Courts reject hearsay, but Suspense revels in it. Suspense is full of big talk, threats, misinformation.

Finally, and in summary, Suspense is about telling lies. You can change the world by telling a lie. You can ruin your life, or save it, by telling a lie. Sometimes the good investigator has to tell lies, has to pretend, in order to get to where he must get to. Lawyers and cops do it all the time. You know what I mean? They cajole, they verbal, they pretend to know or not know. They confuse the witness, or the defendant, in the box because they want to win the case. Truth is always a victim in crime and justice. The crime writer tells lies about the outcome of his story in order to keep the reader hooked, and for the sake of a seductive, winning narrative. That's Suspense. Irresolution until the point of resolution. The artful dodger.

'I think I've done it, Marele. I've hooked a school of red herrings. I've got them all nicely landed.'

'Red herrings, eh?'

'That's right. They're flapping around in the bottom of the bucket now.'

'Why are they red, Mr Krauth? And come to think of it, why are they herrings?'

'Geez, Marele. You really want the whole story, don't you? I looked them up in the dictionary. Red herrings are "elements of an ambiguous indefinite nature, diverting attention from the subject in hand by stating irrelevant but exciting questions." The saying refers to the use of red herrings in exercising hounds. The dogs sniff them and go for broke.'

'Are you suggesting the reader of crime fiction is a dog?'

'Sure, Marele. A bloodhound, I hope.'

'I like dogs, Mr Krauth. I don't want any aspersions cast on dogs. Dogs aren't stupid, Mr Krauth.'

'I wasn't suggesting that, Marele. I was only using the dictionary. I do it all the time.'

'Is that the medical dictionary? What does it say about drinking champagne 24 hours a day?'

'Ah, Marele. That's unfair. Hello? Hello? Are you there?'

So there it is. Case closed. Setting, Action and Suspense. Three bastards you'll have to investigate and come to terms with. Each of them elusive. Each of them capable of much more than you might at first suspect. Each of them key players in the crime story. They each have a hand in it. A big hand. You can't ignore them. And they're all part of the same big syndicate. Suspense does deals with Action and Setting. Setting does deals with Action and Suspense. And so on.

And in a real sense you have no option but to enlist their services, get in on their scams. You won't write a crime story without their cooperation. You won't effectively get to the end of your piece without them as accomplices. Accessories, they are. In the legal sense. Accessories before, during, and after the fact of writing.

I needed to ring Marele again. I wanted my fee. But I also wanted to know who else she had investigating this crime writing business. And what were those other investigators looking at? Character? Plot? Language? Viewpoint? The history of the genre? Minor players. That's what Jean-Pierre (my assistant) and I reckoned. There was nothing else you needed to know to solve the problem of writing crime stories. We'd done it all. Setting, Action and Suspense. They were the prime suspects. Nail them and you could hand the whole lot over to your client and her lawyers. You'd earned your cheque.

'It's in the mail, Mr Krauth.'

'Come on, Marele. I'm not going to fall for that one.'

'You don't believe me?'

'I'd prefer you hand-delivered it. It's my baked beans and caviar. My cheap champagne. You know what I mean? Perhaps I could come around to your place to pick it up.'

'That's out of the question. You'll just have to trust me, won't you?'

'I don't like playing games, Ms Day.'

'Don't you, really? And you call yourself a crime writer?'

It's a difficult business. I still haven't been paid. I've checked out her bank accounts. (There are ways, you know.) She's loaded. I'm not. The electricity's been cut off and the last bottle of Jean-Pierre is sitting hot in the fridge. I'll pop it anyway. The phone's still connected, though.

It's a funny game, crime.

'Hello? Marele?'

'Hi. You've called Marele Day's number. I've just popped out for a while. But if you'd like to leave your name and number and the time of your call, I'll get back to you as soon as I can.'

The beeeeep almost breaks my eardrum. But I can't blame her. She was right all along. You can establish setting, action and suspense just through phone calls. Providing you know what you're doing. And providing your reader knows what you're doing.

Forget the cheap champagne. There are plenty of other cheap tricks available in the crime genre. That's what I meant by passwords and codewords. It's a genre, isn't it? You're halfway there if you obey the rules. But writers get desperate ...

Exercises

Setting
1. Your protagonist's 'home' is an important setting, whether it be an actual dwelling, a pub, an office or other place. Write a description of it. Try to make this description come to life rather than being a real estate inventory. For example, when the investigator opens a drawer to get a piece of paper what else do we see in there— a gun, a bottle of bourbon, a book on allergies?

2. Choose three different types of murder, for example, a domestic, an underworld payback, a political assassination. Write a paragraph describing where, in each case, the murder took place.

Action
1. Write an action scene (a fight or confrontation) from three different points of view—the point of view of the aggressor, the victim, the fly on the wall.

Suspense
1. Suspense is a slow tease that should last the whole of the book. However, as an exercise, write a suspenseful scene. Choose something from a movie, for example, the shower scene in *Psycho*, and put it into words. Focus on the small disturbances, creaking steps, shadows on curtains, characters' reactions to these.

9 THE WORDS ON THE PAGE

Debra Adelaide

Crime fiction is an umbrella for a wide variety of subgenres. Certainly the first-person narrative prevails, as does the hardboiled tone. But not all first-person narrative voices are hardboiled. Some, like Jean Bedford's Anna Southwood, are only softboiled, while others are not boiled at all. Not all heroes are professionals, private eyes. Some, like Robert Wallace's Essington Holt, are propelled into intrigue, mystery and crime by circumstance. Others, like Jennifer Rowe's Verity Birdwood, are amateur sleuths, as self-effacing in personality as they are in their detective methods. And even if the narrators are private eyes, they are not all the wisecracking, sardonic, lonely, hard-drinking stereotypes that have their origins in the fictions of Raymond Chandler and Dashiell Hammett.

Style and subject matter

Given the wide variety of forms available, it's obvious that an equally wide variety of styles will exist. Narratives will range from the terse, pithy and action-packed to the reflective and leisurely, allowing the author to focus much more on the emotional or psychological state of the characters. It is up to the author to choose the style appropriate to the main character and the voice of the text.

The concept of *choosing* a style might initially seem odd. How does one choose a style? Isn't style just a result of the story, something incidental? And doesn't it come naturally, without needing to be thought about?

The answer to this might be yes if you were writing another form of fiction. But if you are writing crime fiction, then, whether you realise it or not, you have elected to write in a particular form, which comes with its own rules, conventions, stereotypes and other attributes.

This doesn't mean you have to adhere to any set of rules or guidelines. Writers who do this risk making the form merely formulaic and the genre dull or even dead. But it does mean that you need to demonstrate some ability to utilise or exploit the conventions. Turning them to original use is a sign of a really good crime writer. One example of this is the recent trend challenging the stereotype of the traditional private eye. What in conventional private eye fiction might be humdrum may, in a female voice and in the hands of a female writer, become fresh, lively, amusing. It may even deliberately send up or invert the gender roles which have traditionally privileged the active freewheeling male over the female.

The opening chapter of Marele Day's debut crime novel, *The Life and Crimes of Harry Lavender*, is a brilliant example of this ability to exploit the conventions. The first-person narrator wakes to a seedy bedroom scene, clearly the result of late-night indulgence in sex, alcohol, cigarettes, and more sex. Clothes and shoes are strewn across the room, the narrator has a hangover, there is a blond asleep in the bed. The narrator takes the obligatory dose of strong black coffee and cold shower, then awakens the sleeping blond before leaving for work:

> 'Time to go sweetheart,' I whispered into the blond's aural orifice. Not a flicker of an eyelid or a murmur. Next time I shook him. 'C'mon mate, wake up. I've got to go to a funeral.'

In offering this witty inversion, the opening also makes promises (which are amply fulfilled as the narrative progresses) of further surprises and challenges to the orthodoxy of the genre. The style is maintained throughout the novel and is appropriate to the narrator, who is wry, active, cynical, somewhat vulnerable, sexual, suspicious and, deep down inside, at the very centre of the hardboiling, a tiny bit soft.

If you are writing, say, a police procedural, in the third person, then this sort of witty, terse style would be inappropriate. The prose style would not need to be lean and sinewy. Jokes and wry observations might come to sound tedious and forced, for the reader would be hearing your voice instead of the voices of the characters. If your narrative is a dense, richly textured one offering fine details of character and convincing psychological insight—such as P.D. James writes—then you would naturally shy away from the style of the freelance private eye.

On the other hand, as the novels of Carl Hiaasen demonstrate, hallmarks like cynicism and terseness can facilitate an essentially satirical approach. This is because Hiaasen writes in the third person, with a shifting point of view which prevents any particular character from dominating the narrative, and this allows us the detachment to collude with his fairly heavy-handed satire. Outrageous things are said; extreme, exaggerated and unbelievable things are claimed, plot-wise and in terms of character. But filtered through the satirical lens, all these things are perfectly acceptable, whereas of course they simply wouldn't work if Hiaasen was writing through the eyes of, say, a Miss Marple or an Adam Dalgleish.

Less is more

Teachers of fiction and editors of manuscripts find themselves saying 'cut' (or actually doing it to manuscripts) more than any other editorial advice or intervention. The urge to say everything, as a writer, is often irresistible. Experienced writers know when to cut because they understand the value of what is *not* said.

The reader, it must be remembered, has a good imagination—probably just as good as the writer's. It is this integration of the imaginative process—this unconscious but powerful dialogue between two minds—which makes the reading experience such an immensely pleasurable and satisfying one. Each reader brings to a book a view that gives that book a special meaning. It is as if the book was written for that one person alone. This is the power of creativity.

As a writer you need to bear in mind that the reader enters into the creative process too. Indeed, it has been argued that a book has no meaning—does not even exist—until a reader begins to read it.

Therefore you need to allow for the imagination of the reader, and this is why you shouldn't spell things out in too much detail. If you do, your reader will be lost to you, for you will be denying his or her rightful role in the creative process. For example, while the reader might need to know certain things about a character's appearance, a very long description ultimately achieves little more than a few effective words.

How many times have you seen the film version of a book, and been disappointed because a particular character has not resembled *your* imagined character, the one you saw so clearly when you read the book? This happens frequently, because despite all attempts an author might make to create a specific appearance for a character, the reader's imagined character is the one that will persist. So there's little virtue in being too specific about appearances, or any other description for that matter. Respect for the creative power of the reader must be become second nature to you as a writer: then you will find understatement and reticence operating automatically as you write.

True and false beginnings

New or inexperienced authors commonly labour over their opening sentences, paragraphs or even pages. While it is true that beginnings are important, it is misguided to think you have to 'introduce' your story or novel in the same way as you might a lecture or essay.

The story, if you allow it to, will tell itself, and if you strain over it the reader will know. Similarly with openings. The true opening will be there if your story has integrity and overall merit. And if you work too hard on the beginning, you may never really start your story; you may get so bogged down in making the opening perfect that the remainder will never get told.

A useful means of circumventing the 'beginning blues' is to go back to your draft and throw away the first page or two, or even the first chapter. I have frequently read manuscripts with tedious beginnings, only to find that the opening of the second chapter, where the author actually gets stuck into the story, is the real beginning of the book. This is what I mean by a true or false beginning: the latter is just added on by the author and, like all sewn-on patches, it shows.

Another helpful technique is to forget all about a beginning and simply start writing the material that is most vivid in your mind. You may find, after completing a first draft, that this will make a suitable beginning after all; or you may decide that it should go near the end of your story; but by then the beginning will have presented itself to you and you will be amazed to find how easily it all fits together.

Here is a good opening:

> Chouette watched from the top of the dutch dresser as George Thurkle dismembered the carcass. Her eyes were as glossy as peeled green grapes, and from the varnished corners of her mouth protruded tiny fangs like garlic cloves. She twitched at each blow as he beat the air from the squealing lungs.

> Helen Simpson, *Flesh and Grass* (1990)

Why is this opening so good? Because of the original and witty use of simile (fangs and garlic cloves having intriguing and sinister connotations); because we're not told directly—only in various sly ways—that Chouette is a cat; because of the graphic violent image which makes us wonder instantly, Is he a butcher? A murderer? (He is neither.) And so on. In short, it hooks us right from the start. And it tells us quite a lot of information without appearing to do so (for instance, the dutch dresser indicates that the setting is a kitchen; there is a strong suggestion about the relationship between the cat and Thurkle).

Here are a few more openings:

> There were two things on Winston's mind as the taxi pulled up outside the narrow terrace in the back streets of Paddington. The first was the promise to his brother that this time he'd do everything he could to go straight. No compromises, no zigzag, just straight. And the second was how he was going to wind up in bed with Mardi Dennehy at the end of the night.

> Steve Wright, 'Winston Goes Straight' (1991)

> She was a neighbour. She was an acquaintance of Dora's and they spoke if they met in the street. Only this time there had been more to it than passing the time of day.

> Ruth Rendell, *An Unkindness of Ravens* (1985)

> 'Jill'
> I challenge the mirror
> 'how much guts have you got?'

> Dorothy Porter, *The Monkey's Mask* (1994)

Wright's opening tells us a great deal in a short space—the main character is fresh out of jail, he has an attitude problem regarding women—and it tells us these things without appearing to do so. Rendell's opening picks us up by the scruff of our neck and sweeps us into the story in an instant.

The quotation from Dorothy Porter was cheating, since to find crime in poetry is such a novelty you'd probably keep reading anyway. Yet it is brisk, bold, challenging, right from the start.

Nifty, deft, funny, intriguing, whatever—a good opening launches straight into the story from the very first line.

Here, by way of contrast, is a poor opening:

> The Hakoah Club in Bondi is a very, very nice club, frequented by very, very nice members and their guests; mainly Eastern suburbs citizens of the Jewish faith. Set where Hall Street rises past the post office, you walk up a small set of wide, white marble steps, through the glass door and into a

cool, bright foyer; reception and phones on the right, door-man and guests' book on the left. The floor then gently rises past a small, angled fountain, set beneath a large copper Menorah candelabrum to take you into the main drinking and dining area. There's a poker-machine room on your left, a bar, a lengthy servery full of choice foods, staffed by polite staff, then a check-out lady and coffee machine next to a large cabinet full of cream-stuffed cakes and other calorie-drenched delicacies.

Robert Barrett, *White Shoes, White Lines and Blackie* (1992)

The description continues for another two lengthy paragraphs, and seems more appropriate to a guide to Sydney clubs than to fiction. It's not exceptionally bad by any means, but the description is far too long for its purpose, which is basically to provide the setting for the main character. There are limits to how much descriptive detail a reader can keep in his or her head, and unless you are familiar with the Hakoah Club, it is unlikely that you will maintain as vivid and detailed an impression of the place as Barrett is giving. Exactly the same impression could have been created in two or three sentences, and without risking the reader's impulse to skip whole passages to get to the substance of the piece.

Endings, by comparison, are relatively easy. So long as all the threads of your story are gathered together, tied up or otherwise accounted for (essential in crime fiction; not so essential in other forms of fiction), then it's usually safe and often actually desirable to allow the narrative simply to stop. Endings in theory can never really ruin a book, because readers would not have got to the final pages if they hadn't enjoyed the ride. By the end, then, you are free to do exactly what you want. But there is one rule that *must* be obeyed: never ever introduce a new character or new material.

Clichés and conventions of crime fiction

As a general rule in writing, clichés are to be avoided like the plague.

See? That is very hard to do.

As another general rule, rules are there to be broken. Or bent judiciously. One of the characteristics of crime writing is that it thrives on the cliché: the wisecracking private eye, the dark mean streets, the sudden, swift thump in the guts, the sweet old lady who uses arsenic, the gun in the small of the back, the hostile police, the car chase: the examples are endless.

But the art of good crime fiction, as opposed to bad pulp (remember, there *is* good pulp), lies in deploying clichés at exactly the right time and using them innovatively. It lies in being able to see the line between useful and even necessary convention on the one hand, and chronically fatigued phraseology on the other. The examples above are clichés of theme; my concern here is clichés of style.

Avoiding the cliché *should* be your brief. Reinventing the cliché *could* be your brief. The overall message of this section might be this: scrutinise your work and delete any clichés, then reward yourself by including a few that you have thought over and carefully polished to make them yours, and no one else's.

For instance, you could take a worn-out phrase such as 'I was on tenterhooks' (and how many people even know what a tenterhook is?) and turn it into something like this: 'I felt like a piece of cloth stretched on a tenter frame: any tauter and I'd rip . . .' This would summon up the cliché without actually using it, as well as tell your reader what exactly being on tenterhooks might be (and if you're not sure by now, look it up in the dictionary). It is also an effective piece of imagery, indicating the immense tension felt by the narrator.

The standard cliché is a phrase or expression which has stuck in the language. It may evoke nothing more than banality. Overuse is its key feature. An author who is lazy, who doesn't pay attention to every word written, may rely on clichés. However, in the right hands, the standard cliché may shine brilliantly, displaying wit and originality, and giving the prose a special lustre.

Clichés, of course, do have value: phrases become clichés because they are useful, because they effectively convey information or images to a wide audience. They are a handy, glib way of uniting us as a group, of expressing a certain kind of truth. Hence their great value in advertising. When we hear the phrase 'the real thing', we now, consciously or not, think of Coca Cola—as do millions of others around the world.

But you are a writer, not an advertiser.

The cliché may be used successfully for a release of tension, for humour, for irony, for anticlimax. The columnist and critic Dorothy Parker, who did pay attention to her language, put clichés to very effective use by inverting or embellishing them. 'Another drink,' she said, 'and I'll be under the host.'

Here are some poor examples of the use of clichés:

He was as cunning as a shithouse rat.
Silent sobs racked her breast as she prayed fervently.
I vowed to move heaven and earth to find the girl.
Inwardly she seethed with conflicting emotions.
He had been a tower of strength these last few months.

There's nothing intrinsically wrong with any of these phrases, except that they have been used again and again until they no longer have any significance. Offering a clever, bright, lively cliché rather than a tired old one is like giving a newly-minted coin to the reader. It delights and thrills, however briefly, and that is important in fiction.

Here are some judicious examples of the use of cliché:

> I was on a strict diet, but she aimed the sugar dispenser at my cup in a determined manner. 'Go ahead,' I said, 'make my day.'

> (unpublished manuscript)

> I hoped I wasn't going to get run over. It might be all right for Dolores, but I didn't want to be seen dead wearing mock-alligator ankle boots.

> Marele Day, *The Last Tango of Dolores Delgado* (1992)

Often the right placement of a cliché can make it work: this is what I mean by using clichés judiciously. They can be used parodically (as in the first example, which relies on a wide common knowledge of popular films), or mockingly, as in the second example, where the phrase's literal meaning is cleverly exploited.

When tempted to use a cliché ask yourself: Do I really know what this means? ('mordant humour' and 'blatantly obvious' are just two examples of phrases in constant use whose exact meaning eludes many). Do I really need to use this cliché? Is this the best way to express my meaning? Does my reader really need to read this phrase yet again?

The answers to all these questions should be 'no'. 'Rosy-fingered dawn' was OK when Homer used it, but it's lost some of its sheen over the centuries. And as for night following day, or the old harsh realities, remember you're a writer, not a politician.

Adjectives and adverbs

These are the cockroaches of fiction. Just as every household has to have a few cockroaches, so every piece of fiction will have its adjectives and adverbs. They can never be completely exterminated, so the best approach is to learn to live with them amicably.

I'm not against adjectives and adverbs, only their overuse or clumsy use. Deleting adjectives occupies a considerable proportion of manuscript editors' time. It gives authors a lot of pain, but the result is a vastly improved piece of writing.

During composition lessons in primary school, my teacher would write the following prohibited words in large letters on the blackboard: SUDDENLY, GREAT and SCARY. On a particularly bad day she would add GHOSTLY, FRIGHTENING and HUGE. I don't know if she suspected she was nursing a batch of incipient Gothic horror writers, or if all primary children tended to overuse these adverbs and adjectives when given their head, but each week we were faced with the challenge of writing a story without these words, to us the most vivid in the language.

Now, as an editor, I can appreciate the reasoning behind the teacher's lists. She wanted to force us to think originally, to be genuinely creative, and not to *rely* on certain words and phrasing to carry meaning. One of my favourite pieces of advice comes from the late journalist Ross Campbell. He said:

I have been told that I'm an economical writer and I think
it is true that I try not to waste words and I do go through
and frequently cut out words. I'm inclined to cut out adjectives and adverbs if they don't seem to be serving any purpose.
I think I may have picked up that idea from reading that
Maupassant used to go through his short stories and remove
all the adjectives.

While I would not recommend Maupassant's method to the
letter, I would certainly recommend the spirit of Campbell's
approach. As with clichés, you can always reward yourself after
picking out the adjectives by putting a few back in. You will
be surprised, however, to find just how reluctant you'll be to
do this, after having read your new, leaner, more economical
piece of writing.

Economy is important in crime writing, especially in those
subgenres where the focus is less on mood, theme and place,
and more on action, event and character.

The poetics of the language

There is no magic or mystery to the art of writing. However,
a good piece of writing is full of magic and mystery, which is
why readers want to keep reading it. Finding the natural
rhythm of your prose style is one of your most important tasks
as a fiction writer.

Because crime fiction is a genre with readily identifiable
characteristics, it is very tempting to copy the style of other
authors, especially if you are writing a first-person private eye
narrative. Even if you are not consciously tempted to copy, you
may do so unconsciously. But only Raymond Chandler wrote
like Raymond Chandler, and while the influence of his style
(understated, cool, darkly witty, etc) may be inescapable, your
task is to create a unique voice for yourself and your main
character.

You may emulate an approach yet not copy any set of
characteristics. Since I mentioned Chandler, we may as well
look at something by him that illustrates why he was such a
successful writer.

It was about eleven o'clock in the morning, mid-October, with the sun not shining and a look of hard wet rain in the clearness of the foothills. I was wearing my powder-blue suit, with dark blue shirt, tie and display handkerchief, black brogues, black wool socks with dark blue clocks on them. I was neat, clean, shaved and sober, and I didn't care who knew it. I was everything the well-dressed private detective ought to be. I was calling on four million dollars.

Raymond Chandler, *The Big Sleep* (1939)

This is a very famous passage from a classic, the opening paragraph in fact. What makes it such a splendid piece of writing? You might notice the use of such devices as contrast (hard wet rain/clearness of the foothills), the gentle playing with reader expectation (the sun not shining), and of course the dry humour. But most of all this piece is so effective because of the *rhythm* of the prose as it unfolds to that last sentence. Chandler builds up this rhythm through the repetition of words like 'blue' (he does it later in the novel with 'grey') and of the phrase 'I was' which starts four of the five sentences here (the other starts with a variation on it: 'It was'). The two opening sentences are straightforward and logical descriptions, clearly placing a character in a well-defined world, while the third undercuts this bland logic with its inversion of expectations (' . . . and I didn't care who knew it'). The final sentence is fairly short, sharp, to the point, neatly rounding off the paragraph.

The descriptive matter in this piece may seem to refute my earlier point about unnecessary detail, but a close look will reveal that this is not so. Chandler is deliberately going into detail to send his character up, or rather the narrative voice of Philip Marlowe is sending itself up. The whole point of the careful details (the powder-blue suit, the brogues, the socks with their blue clocks) is to be found in that brilliant sentence, 'I was neat, clean, shaved and sober, and I didn't care who knew it.' A great deal about the character is suggested this way: normally he's not neat, clean, or sober; he's self-conscious and self-mocking; he's laconic, drily witty, and so on. The overall tone is one of confidence—the confidence of a character who knows what he's about, and, importantly, the confidence of an author with every syllable of the prose under control.

If you tried to copy this, your readers would know it. If, however, you examine why writers like Chandler are so good by looking closely at their prose, you will come to understand some fundamental facts about language and style.

Strong sentence structure is crucial, and is rarely learned instinctively. You need to work hard on the hiatus which always exists between what is in your head and what appears on the page. Sometimes the two can be very different. Problematic pieces of writing can often be sorted out by asking yourself, What, exactly, am I trying to say? Then why didn't I say it like that?

Many people think there is something known as literary writing (even for a 'low' genre such as crime fiction), and that this is what distinguishes 'literature' from other forms of writing (on the backs of cereal packets, for instance). This misconception makes new authors think they have to write in a florid, wordy, adjective-riddled, complex style.

In fact there is no such thing as literary writing. There is only good writing and bad writing, despite the genre. Bad writing makes boring reading. You may not know why you dislike something, you'll just know that you don't want to keep reading it.

But by investigating these 'poetics' of language, you will acquire a vocabulary which will not only make you recognise poor writing and understand why it is poor, but also equip you to be a better writer.

You also need to undersand the logic of prose structure. For this you will need to scrutinise your work sentence by sentence, pretending, if you can, that you are not its author at all, but some hard-nosed critic able to sniff out inconsistencies of thought and logic.

One sentence should always follow another. That may seem to be stating the obvious, but it is very easy to get sidetracked, even in the space of a paragraph. If, for instance, you're in the middle of describing the evening sky, don't interrupt to tell us that the phone was ringing before going back to explain that it looked as if it was about to rain.

Reading early drafts aloud to yourself can be an effective way of identifying weak spots in your writing. Things you suspect might sound silly very often do. And if they sound silly to you, imagine how they would sound to the reader. As far as sentence structure goes, reading aloud is extremely useful. If you find you cannot read a sentence from beginning to end without taking several deep breaths, like a swimmer approaching the 100-metre mark, then it's quite likely your sentence is too long. Oh no, I hear you say: readers aren't reading aloud, so it doesn't matter. And Henry James wrote sentences that went on for nearly a page.

My answer to these objections is that readers unconsciously 'listen' for the natural cadences of speech in the written word and will shy away from stilted and overlong sentences.

And as for James, more people read P.D. than Henry.

Truth versus believability

Just as important as tackling structural logic is dealing with the problem of literal truth. Fiction writers are magicians and inventors. Crime fiction writers are utterly dependent on coincidence and improbability. But there is a point beyond which the real, hard, actual, verifiable truth may never be stretched. Again, the line here is a fine one. A small example will do (and here I'm speaking in terms of style, not plot, which is another realm of truth versus believability altogether). When Kinky Friedman says, in *Frequent Flyer* (1989), 'I felt hot pain mingling with cold fear,' one might be inclined to scepticism. Does pain feally feel hot? Does fear feel cold, or like anything at all? But Friedman continues: 'The two sensations seemed to alternate rapidly, kind of like taking a hotel shower in Mexico.' In this instance the humour not only takes the edge off the violence being described at this point, but also works against the sensations described above. If the author was offering a straight, serious narrative (with Friedman, a conceptual impossibility) then the description of hot pain and cold fear might just seem overdone or unrealistic.

Peter Corris writes:

> I walked over to my car, opened the door and dropped into the seat. I knew at once that something was wrong. There was something missing and something was there that shouldn't have been. I put the key in the ignition in a reflex action and then jet engines roared in my ears and an oil refinery exploded in my skull. Cascades of sparks and glowing concentric circles flared and died.

Peter Corris, White Meat (1981)

Here Corris is consciously exploiting the convention. We expect—in a certain type of first person, private eye narrative—that the narrator will experience some form of physical violence. It's impossible to tread the mean streets without encountering it. So in every Cliff Hardy tale, Cliff gets beaten up, knocked out or assaulted in one way or another.

In the above passage, we know that an oil refinery did not literally explode in Cliff's skull. The over-exaggeration does two things. It reassures us that the narrative is under control by consciously, or even self-consciously, invoking a convention of the genre. And it reassures us that Cliff Hardy will survive not only this incident, but the whole novel, to tell us another tale. (Of course, we also know that from the fact that he is telling us the tale, but here author and reader conspire together and really have done from page 1; if we are overly critical of the first-person narrative, then we shouldn't be bothering to read in the first place, in fact if this is the case we are not readers so much as voyeurs.)

On the other hand, an anonymous student of mine, along with thousands of others, once wrote: 'Her heart skipped a beat.' When I read something like this I ask myself, Is this literally true? Do I believe it really occurred?

The answer is no. This may seem like nitpicking, because we could argue that we *know* what the writer means, so it's all right in places to stretch the truth. Had that student, or any of the other writers who've used this phrase, followed this claim with an ironic, humorous undercutting, as Friedman does above, then the reader would be prepared to accept the fictional truth of the statement.

Another student wrote: 'She barely made it to the door on legs that refused to function.' Again, we get the general idea, but if you look closely you can see that this is literally impossible. If her legs refused to function she couldn't make it to the door on them, barely or otherwise. Choose your words carefully; make sure they say exactly what you mean them to say.

Rewriting, rewriting, rewriting

I offer all these suggestions to make some aspects of your writing and rewriting easier, but be warned: rewriting is rarely easy. Usually the prose that reads the smoothest is the prose that has undergone six or ten drafts. And tackling full-scale structural problems, which might involve moving large chunks of material back and forth, can be extremely difficult. Nevertheless, there is a point where if your story has strength and integrity (to put it bluntly, if it's a worthy one after all), then these fundamental virtues will sooner or later prevail. Then you will find it's a matter of fine tuning, and it's at this point that you might find some of the above useful.

Exercises

1. Write a one-page description of anything at all (people at a party, a dog fight). Take a different coloured pen and remove all the adjectives but two. Reread the new piece. Does it still work or not? If you can't decide, give it to a disinterested person and ask them. If you decide it does work, replace some adjectives—if you can.

2. Photocopy a passage, paragraph or page that appeals to
    you from one of your favourite crime writers. Go through
    it with a pen, marking features like long and short senten-
    ces, highlighting descriptive words and imagery, and exam-
    ining such things as the opening words of sentences. Look
    for repetition and variation of words or sounds, with an
    eye to discovering the underlying rhythms and patterns
    within the prose. Now see if you can explain to yourself
    why the piece works so well, and why the author appeals
    to you.

10 FROM ROUGH IDEA TO FINAL DRAFT

Jean Bedford

I will begin with a very generalised description of the life of a hypothetical detective novel, from the first thought that you might like to write one, to the finished draft you might submit to a publisher or agent. What I will say is meant as a guideline only—you may find all of it interesting and useful, or none of it. Everyone has his or her own approach to writing a novel as well as to rewriting and editing drafts, and you will, with experience, find the one that you are most comfortable with. It may bear no resemblance whatever to the approaches I describe here, but if it works, if it results in a publishable final draft, then it's right for you.

If you are one of those natural storytellers who need only write one draft, with a minimum of changes, it is likely that much of the rewriting and editing process I will discuss occurs within your subconscious while you write. The rest of us must conscientiously and consciously go through the grind of re-arranging, deleting, adding and changing until we get a draft that fulfils the potential of our original concept.

Some stories arrive full-grown, almost complete in their detail and organisation. I know one successful detective writer who says the plot unfolds like a film in front of his eyes while he works. He simply writes down what he sees happening. Most stories, however, start with perhaps one or two incidents, or one or two characters, with not much more than a vague idea of a potential narrative. Or they can start with a situation, maybe a moral dilemma or a theory of behaviour. But first of all, there is the feeling that you would like to write a detective novel.

Protagonist

Let's say that our hypothetical 'average' detective novel starts with a character. Perhaps you want to write a novel with a particular sort of person as protagonist and you have thought a lot about this sort of person. Perhaps she or he is based on someone you know, or know of. You have decided on your protagonist's race, sex (and sexual preference), age, profession, tastes, marital status and habits. You know what he or she looks like—how tall, how thin or fat, whether dark or fair; you have a very clear picture of this person, as clear as if he or she were actually someone you knew.

You will have thought seriously about your narrative voice and point of view—whether it will be first-person (traditional in the private eye novel) or third-person, or told from several characters' viewpoints.

You will also understand that the genre you have chosen will prescribe certain things about your character. You may reject these prescriptions, but you should certainly be aware of them, and you should be even more aware of your clear reasons for rejecting them. Usually, your protagonist will be a loner of some sort—divorced, widowed, even a monk (like Ellis Peters's Brother Cadfael). This is almost a prerequisite for the genre, though there are many notable exceptions. Ed McBain's Steve Carella, for example, is happily married (police protagonists seem to get away with this more than private eyes), and Jonathan Kellerman's psychiatrist, Alex Delaware, usually has a significant other, although his relationships (particularly his most serious one) are often fraught. But basically the genre expects, and your readers expect, in one way or another, a lone avenger, a single individual dedicated to the pursuit of justice or at least answers. This does not, of course, mean that your protagonist can't have sexual or emotional adventures and commitments along the way—in fact it's almost required.

In a private eye novel, though not necessarily in other types of detective fiction, your character should also be on the edge financially—hungry for work and a dollar. Again, there are many notable exceptions to this (Margery Allingham's Albert Campion, Dorothy Sayers's Lord Peter Wimsey, Agatha Christie's Miss Marple, and so on), but it's not a bad rule to keep in mind. And I would argue that the exceptions are on the edge in ways that compensate for not being financially needy.

Your character should also be someone the reader can feel sympathy, or at least empathy, for. This character is the tour guide for the adventure your readers are embarking on—he or she must be someone they trust. This doesn't mean your protagonist must be the soul of rectitude—some of the most endearing detectives in literature have been rogues and even criminals, but there is always some element of integrity or heroism or compassion that the reader can identify with and admire. Your readers need to care for your characters, which means that first you must care for them, too.

So, you have your protagonist. He or she conforms, or deliberately does not conform, to genre expectations. Now, perhaps, you need a plot.

Plot ideas

Where do plots come from? This is the question that is most asked of published writers, yet if you are genuinely a writer, or a potential writer, the answer is obvious—they come from everywhere. The world is full of plots; your own life is full of plots, as is your imagination. You may spend your entire life in a country vicarage and write *Wuthering Heights*. Storytelling is intrinsic to being human. We constantly construct stories out of our lives and the lives of people we know or have only heard of. We are incapable, as a species, of *not* telling stories. But as writers, we choose to tell the significant stories, the ones others will want to be told and the ones we need to tell. If you don't feel this *need* to tell your stories to a wider audience than your immediate circle, then you might as well stop now—you are not a writer.

Many detective writers conceive their plots from an incident they read about in the papers, or hear about on the news. Gabrielle Lord based her thriller *Fortress* on a real incident in which a group of children and their teacher were abducted and held hostage. She combined her own imaginings about the situation, how people cope with such ordeals, with other personal preoccupations—with courage and defiance and what individuals are capable of under great stress—to make a novel. It was a story she needed to tell and that a wide audience wanted to read.

The plot idea for my first detective novel, *Worse Than Death*, came from a report I read in the paper about a woman who went to prison for years for kidnapping her daughter from her husband—a man who habitually abused the child yet had gained custody of her. It made me think about the sorts of sacrifice we are capable of making for our children, and that, married to ideas I already held about child abuse and parental power, led to a story I thought was worth telling.

In general, then, your plots may come from anything in the world around you, but they will usually illustrate something you already feel the urge to say. When you can ask yourself, What is this story about? and give yourself a clear and concise answer, you have a viable plot idea. Your answer may be one word—lust, power, jealousy, fear, hatred. It may be a phrase or a sentence—the abuse of power; what happens when love turns to hatred; what negative childhood influences will do to someone; how people cope with loss, and so on. In either case, it will be concise. If you don't know what your story is about, it will be very difficult for your readers to make a guess. If you do know, in this sense, what your story is about, then you will have a valid focus for the necessary workings of your plot/s. It will also be useful to have thought in this way when you are asked to provide a synopsis for a publisher, or, when your book is accepted, to draft a back-cover blurb. The actual plotting, the storyline—who does what to whom, how, when and why—

is the vehicle by which you reveal what you are writing about, and this evolves from what you believe, imagine, read, observe, hear or experience.

Plot conventions

Before we move on to talk about making plot outlines, we should look at some general aspects of the detective plot, as some of the traditional exigencies of the genre can be useful to the beginning writer. Fortunately, there are certain accepted procedural guidelines that you can use. Of course, if you are confident enough, you can choose to ignore them as well, but as in any art, you must understand what you are rejecting and why.

The plots of most detective stories proceed in similar ways, with similar preconceptions (we have already discussed some of the preconceptions about the character of the protagonist). Even where these preconceptions have been deliberately discarded or played around with, as in some recent 'postmodernist' or 'experimental' or 'cross-genre' examples (notably, in Australia, in the work of Jan McKemmish, Brenda Walker, Finola Moorhead and Dorothy Porter), I would argue that they are still strongly embedded, even if negatively, in the text.

For a start, usually the most important thing has *already happened*. This may be the central incident of the plot—the main murder, or set of murders—or it may be a salient occurrence (or sequence of occurrences) in the remote or recent past which has led up to the story now being told. This *important thing* may be revealed at once, as in the classic private eye novel, where a client appears with a specific problem, or it may not be revealed until the very end of the novel, when strands from the past finally emerge to create a pattern, but it will always have happened essentially before your story begins.

Second, something great must be at stake—preferably life itself—for either the protagonist or another main character. It can be the life of the client, or, in less traditional plots, the life of a loved one of the protagonist, but there must be real and present danger. For me, personally, the best detective novels play for the greatest stakes: they must centre on murder, and there must be at least the threat of more murder to come.

Third, there should be significant obstacles to overcome in what is essentially the detective's quest. These obstacles can take the form of red herrings and spurious but convincing alternative suspects, as in the clue-puzzle mystery; or lies and threats of physical violence, as in the more hardboiled novels, but they must be real and convincing. The skeleton of your plot, upon which every other element depends for success, is the recounting of *how* these obstacles are overcome and the problem/mystery solved. Your job, here, is to show your readers, against all the odds, why the crimes have been, or are being, committed, and by whom.

Fourth, the mystery should be solved and justice should be done or seen to be done. This does not necessarily mean that the culprit answers to the law for his or her crime. There is a long tradition of the perpetrator escaping legal justice yet still being satisfactorily punished or made to pay. There is also a long tradition of the immediate culprit being caught but the malaise that produced the crime continuing—corruption in high places, untouchable principals, the abuse of money and power. Even here, however, we should come away with the sense that some blow, even if a small, insignificant one, has been struck against evil. When the criminal appears to have escaped justice, he or she is usually clearly in line for some other, perhaps worse, punishment. There is a recent trend that even leaves the mystery unsolved on this level—that is, the protagonist never fully finds out what has happened and why—but resolves a deeper mystery, to do with character and motive, instead.

Plot outline

Some writers make elaborate plot outlines and stick to them, chapter by chapter. Robert B. Parker, the creator of the Spenser series, makes highly detailed chapter outlines—almost synopses of each chapter—before he begins his first draft.

Others simply have a broad idea of what their story is about (perhaps only our one-word answer) and let what they write define what they will write next. Others use various combinations of these methods.

My own version of making a plot outline and sticking to it is to begin with a fairly general synopsis of the main plot and the various subplots. I write a short and simple account of what the central crime is and who has committed it and why. Then I write a more elaborate set of notes about the *apparent* circumstances of the crime—that is, how the situation will be presented to my detective. This will include the red herrings and any other obstacles to solving the mystery. I make a list of main characters, with their personal details—age, sex, looks, physical characteristics, relationships to each other. I try to sketch out the main changes of action and direction, which will provide the basis for chapters. I often end up discarding or ignoring a great deal of this, but I always plot (or re-plot) ahead in some detail while I am writing.

Other writers do none of this. Some see where their writing leads them and rely on rewriting to fix any glaring inconsistencies or fill any gaps. Others write very broad outlines of the major action and make up everything else as they go along. Some start with an idea and a character and not much else and see where that leads them. Agatha Christie said that she always wrote the final chapter first so she'd know who'd done it and why, then she plotted the rest of the book. I have heard of writers who put descriptions and pieces of action on file cards, then toss them in the air and let where they fall determine the sequence of their plot. There is no right or wrong way to approach writing your novel, only the way that works for you. I feel safe if I know in advance the main events; other writers are bored by knowing everything that will happen. With experience, you will find out which sort of writer you are.

The first draft

This is where no one else can really help you. Like childbirth and death, writing is something you must do alone. However, a couple of points about where you begin and how you find your voice might be helpful.

How do you find the right way in to your novel? Sometimes you're lucky and the first chapter you write remains the first chapter. More often, you will find at revision stage that the first few pages are tentative and not really working. What we discussed before about the exigencies of the genre can help you here. You know that the important thing has already happened. So your first necessity is to inform your protagonist (and the reader) about the immediate consequence of this important thing—that is, the crime that apparently needs to be solved. The best advice I can give you about starting a detective novel is to leap straight in. Detective novels are, almost by definition, action novels—your readers want action, and they want it now. Then they want more. Introduce your protagonist, then bring him or her immediately up against the problem that will occupy most of the plot. Again, with experience, you will be able to play around with this, but it is a good rule to follow when you are starting.

Finding your voice is a different matter—there aren't really any rules that will comfort you. It may take several drafts before you are satisfied with the voice/s of your novel, or you may hit upon the authentic one straight away. Beginning writers often don't find the assured voice of their novel until several chapters in—this is one of the things you will be looking hard at when you come to revise your first draft. Don't let it hold you back from writing, though—you will usually realise when you have hit your stride with voice, and you can go back later and fix up early false notes.

Now it's really up to you. You must simply *write*, and then write some more, then more after that. It's hard work, the muse is flighty and unreliable, and you might wait for years between her visits. So it is important to find a work discipline that suits you and to stick to it. Write as much as you can in every work session—whether that's every day or twice a week, or all night for two weeks and all morning for the next month.

All writers have their own work habits. Some keep office hours and take morning tea and lunch breaks; others write for two hours a day, every day; some (like me) work in fits and starts, with perhaps a fortnight of intensive daily writing and then a week's break (or longer). Robert Ludlum sets himself a definite word limit for each work session and stops when he reaches it, even if he's halfway through a sentence. (Raymond Chandler, when told of this, said he'd never want to read a book by someone who wrote like that.) Ernest Hemingway always left off at a point when he knew what was going to happen next, which I have found a useful tactic. But the important thing is to get words on pages and to keep getting them on. It's probably unproductive to revise your work *within* a work session, but you may wish to read over what you have written in the previous session before you go on. Some people don't read over their work until they've finished a draft, but I suspect they end up with a lot of fussy revision of details. Or their editor does.

There are various possible approaches to your first draft, and you will find the one that suits you. Some of the lucky instinctive story-builders among us will only ever write one draft, and it will be the first and final one, needing no more than some peripheral tinkering at the end to make it publishable. But most of us will need to go through some process of drafting and re-drafting.

Subsequent drafts: A revision checklist

Many writers grimly persevere until they have a finished draft, even when they know there are things wrong, or inconsistencies, or gaps in what they have written. Perhaps they will make notes as they go, as a guideline to rewriting; perhaps they will hope that the problems will simply go away once they have written the final sentence. They don't. Usually some degree of revision should occur during the writing of your first draft, but not so much that it impedes your writing new material.

My own approach is to take incrementally larger steps backward for each step I go forward. I rework everything I have written in my previous work session before I write anything new. This often means, as the manuscript accumulates, that I have to rework things from sessions before that as well.

I keep running notes about anything or anybody that didn't arise out of my original plot outline (which is, by halfway through the novel, usually a beacon of lucidity and logic desperately glimpsed from within the impenetrable muddle I seem to have achieved). These notes often lead to subplots, or at least twists of the plot, that I had not anticipated. This, in turn, necessitates going back even further to seed their beginnings, or to delete things that are no longer relevant.

I check events and characters against a timeline and a list of characters and their attributes as I write—though I still find inconsistencies in the final version, and publishers' editors find even more after that. I try to correct grammar, punctuation and spelling and to keep an eye on words overused or repeated. During this process I delete far more than I add, usually finding that in thoughtless moments I've over-explained or used irrelevant dialogue which leads nowhere. I try to keep several questions in mind as I check what I have written: What is the main story (the 'truth')? is the most important one, and What is at stake? What is the desired outcome and how will the detective reach it? What events, information, false assumptions, wild goose chases, will stand in the detective's way? How will the detective overcome these obstacles? I also try to keep in mind the elements of at least one major subplot, even when new ones are springing out at me all over the place.

At final draft stage I usually repeat the whole process for the finished story. This is an obsessive's way of writing, and I don't necessarily recommend it.

Assuming that your approach will be the more common one of completing a draft and then revising, it is still essential that you come to rewriting focused on your central intentions. Ask yourself if it is clear who did what to whom, what they did to conceal it, how your protagonist discovers the truth, and whether the culprit/s will be brought to justice (and if so, what sort of justice). Does the story fulfil its original intention? Is it clear what it is about? You must also ask yourself practical, craft questions: Does the dialogue serve to move the plot along, illuminate the action or reveal character and relation-ship? Or is it a filler, repeating what we already know, and irrelevant to the plot? Are your characters believable? Is their behaviour consistent?

If you have set out to write a clue-puzzle mystery, or a version of one, you will, at draft stage, need to answer a specific set of questions:

- Is my character's voice authentic from the beginning, or will I have to rewrite the early pages to bring it in line with the surer voice later on?
- Is the point of view consistent—that is, is it clear what is the authorial voice and what is the voice of characters?
- Have I provided a credible group of suspects?
- Have I provided enough *fair* clues for the readers to solve the mystery, while at the same time salting enough red herrings to make it unlikely that they will? Has the detective/protagonist reached the solution by fair means—that is, has he or she used the same clues given to the reader to solve the mystery? Or, heaven forbid, has the detective kept back relevant information or given false clues without indicating to the reader that they are not to be relied on?
- Are all loose ends tied off?
- Is the perpetrator, finally, the only person about whom it is completely credible, in terms of character, motivation and opportunity, that he or she committed the crime?

You should have asked yourself these questions during your plotting, of course, but you can answer them more adequately when you have a draft in front of you.

If you are writing a more mainstream detective novel—police procedural, legal or psychological thriller, tough guy private eye story and so on—the same questions might still apply. (Many detective novels are a combination of the clue-puzzle and the hardboiled subgenres.) But your emphasis will probably be different, and the classical components of the clue-puzzle—the limited group of suspects, the red herrings, the misleading subplot/s and the final solving of a sort of cryptic intellectual game—will not provide your overriding criteria. You may need to place more weight on other questions as well:

- What is at stake, or at risk?
- What are the obstacles to overcome?
- Is the outcome dramatically satisfying?
- Are the characters psychologically and emotionally believable? Does the plot follow inevitably from their personalities and behaviour, or their past?
- Does the protagonist (private eye, lawyer, member of the police, journalist, psychiatrist, whatever) reach the solution by detecting? That is, does he or she *investigate* people, motives, relationships, opportunity, past and present events?
- Does the protagonist bring knowledge, experience and expertise to the investigation?
- Does he or she invite the reader to share the action by revealing methods, deductions, assumptions, doubts, analyses?
- Is the protagonist a sympathetic character with whom the reader will want to share this experience?

Again, all these questions can also apply in differing levels of importance to the clue-puzzle mystery, and they are all questions that you will have asked at some level while plotting.

One supremely important question you should ask at this stage, and which may not have occurred to you during the initial plotting, is: *Is everything written here necessary?* The answer, unfortunately, will often be no. Segments of dialogue, description, sometimes complete characters and whole scenes, even your personal favourites, may have to go out the window, if you are honest.

In a detective novel, perhaps more stringently than in more general fiction, every word, scene, piece of dialogue, character (however minor) and event must be absolutely necessary to the plot. Detective novels, whatever subgenre they belong to, are essentially plot-driven, and the requirements of the plot dictate everything you write. No matter if your character makes an amusing digression that scintillates with wit and insight—if it doesn't work somehow to move the plot along, to underline it, initiate action, provide context or illustrate motive or character, then hit the delete button.

The same with dialogue. Dialogue is not conversation, nor is it something useful to fill in gaps between scenes. It is a codified version of human speech which works in fiction to reveal character, emotion, relationship, motive, irony, action, history, previously unknown information. It should not reiterate what the reader already knows, unless to cast new light on it, nor should it be aimless talk. It should always fulfil a distinct purpose in the plot.

Description, too, should perform a function. It need not move the plot along, as such, but it should add texture, provide a context for character, or supply an appropriate (or contrasting) background to action. Sometimes descriptions of places can make those places almost characters in their own right, enhancing the reader's perceptions of the lives of the human characters in the novel. Ask yourself constantly, *Why is that there?* If you can't find an adequate answer, get rid of it.

The above is, if you like, the macro grid against which you will check your draft. It covers the big general questions that should all have been implicit in the writing process—what is sometimes called structural editing. This may seem like a daunting number of things to look for, but many of them will be dealt with on an instinctive level as you read, without conscious thought. They are also the questions that a professional editor will automatically address, so it will save time and torment if you don't shirk them yourself.

On the micro level (copy editing), the process of editing and rewriting your draft will not be very different from that which applies to any other kind of writing. For your purposes, as the writer, the copy editing can take place simultaneously with your structural examination of the draft, though in a publishing house they are usually treated as separate stages.

First, you will need to look for *consistency*—of character, time, plot, movement, chronology and so on. A character introduced as a bit of a bimbo should not suddenly begin talking like an intellectual unless the bimbo aspect has been a ploy, a pose deliberately adopted by the character for believable reasons. Characters may develop and change during the story, but only as a result of their experience, not of authorial carelessness. On a more detailed level, you should check that physical descriptions remain consistent—remember whether people are fair or dark, tall or short, have a limp or waddle, are old or young.

Check the time span of the story. If it goes on over weeks or years, make sure things occur at the right intervals and in the right sequence. If it was Saturday yesterday, it must be Sunday today. If the narrative began in winter and three months have passed, it must now be spring or early summer. If you are the sort of writer who includes the natural landscape, make sure you have the right seasonal flowers in bloom. Never underestimate your readers' knowledge. That very obscure detail that you didn't think worth checking will almost certainly be the one that readers write to your publisher about, or that a reviewer will mention.

Your plot, and your subplots, must be consistent. Check who is related to whom, who knew whom when, who knows what and who is kept in the dark, how facts are discovered, and by whom, when things occurred and who was present and therefore has knowledge of them.

The movements of your characters must be consistent. Someone described as a passenger in a car should not get out of the driver's seat when the journey is over. A character who leaves her reading glasses at home should not put them on to read something a few pages later. A scene begun in a restaurant should not end in a bar, unless the transition from one place to another has been deliberate and described.

Your chronology should be checked for consistency. If a character was born in 1946, he or she will be 50 in 1996. It is useful to make a chart of characters' ages, years of birth, etc. to help you keep track of your chronology. It is also useful to keep a timeline of world, national and local events during the action of the novel, if it spans a few years. This way you can be sure that your 60-year-old in 1995 could not have fought in the Second World War, but might have gone to Vietnam.

At this stage you also check your grammar, spelling and syntax, as well as your vocabulary. Your characters may speak and think ungrammatically, but you, the writer, may not. Be as accurate with spelling as possible (use a dictionary), especially with place names, brand names, makes of automobile, etc.

Make sure your syntax is varied and appropriate—an uneducated gangster is unlikely to use complicated sentences and obscure words. Check that all your sentences do not have the same structure or begin in the same way. (I once edited a novel in which every second paragraph began with 'meanwhile'. It was very irritating to read.) Particularly look for sentences that begin with subordinate clauses—for example, 'Crossing the room, he drew out his gun,' rather than 'He drew out his gun as he crossed the room.' I single this structure out because it is generally overused by beginning writers of fiction. It has its place, but not very often. It distances readers from the action and slows the pace—the last thing you want in a novel of suspense. Check for unnecessary verbiage (too many adjectives detract from description; use just enough enhance it). Ask yourself always, *What is necessary?* Check passages of dialogue to make sure it is clear who is speaking at any given time. Examine your vocabulary and your soul for any discriminatory language that does not arise from the specific attitude of a character. It is all right for your characters to be racist or sexist or homophobic, but you, the writer, should not be. (Nor should you appear to condone such attitudes.) Make sure particular words and images are not overused (use a thesaurus). Again, this seems like a lot to keep in your head, but you will find that you deal with many of these things automatically as you read over your work.

Editing the dramatic structure

The dramatic structure of your novel as a whole is something you should have worked out in your initial plotting. This should be checked as part of structural editing, when you read your draft for revision, but for me it is often the very last thing I look at. You may choose to look at it at any stage you like. Perhaps I leave it till last because I am so afraid there will be a problem with it. Perhaps I have left discussing it till last now because it is such an amorphous and difficult concept.

There are classical rules for dramatic structure which we have already glanced at in a different context. They are: the set-up (statement of problem), the explication and working out (obstacles to overcome), the climax two-thirds of the way through, then the resolution (solution) and after that, perhaps, the anticlimax (the winding down or the postscript). Personally, I am attracted to this approach. But it is possible to successfully change the order around and you can dispense with the idea of one cathartic climax altogether and still achieve a book with a strong and viable structure. That's what makes it so hard to discuss structure in any general way—it's tempting to say that the structure of a novel either works or it doesn't.

Perhaps the most important thing is that *you* understand the structure you were aiming for and that you are able to look at the structure of your first draft with an uncompromising eye. Did you really intend all the action to happen in the last ten pages? Was it deliberate that the main characters went on a peaceful vacation for two chapters halfway through the most exciting and suspenseful part of the plot? Did you really mean to reveal the identity of the perpetrator in Chapter 3 and for the rest of the novel to be an anticlimax? Only you can answer these questions, and only you can present a justification when a publisher's editor asks them.

This is also where you may find you need to move slabs of material around—a frustrating task, but much easier in these days of computers than the old cut-and-paste method. You may realise that your structure is too linear, that you don't want the reader just to follow along from one thing to the next, so you may want to shift some information to later, make some scenes flashbacks, or leap some altogether. Or you may realise that your scenes don't follow each other sequentially and that some transition scenes are needed, or that they have to be reorganised in a different sequence. Don't be afraid of shuffling your material around like this—it is a mechanical task and much easier than it sounds. It can also make a huge difference. You can always change it back again if it doesn't work. Don't worry too much if you have a vague feeling that this sort of reshuffling might be necessary, but you don't see quite where to do it. If your novel works on other levels, the publisher's editor will make suggestions along these lines.

Finally, keep detailed notes of where you need to make revisions. I always edit my work on hard copy (printed out on paper), so I use Post-It notes and write comments on the facing blank pages where I need to delete, add, shift around. If you are one of those people who can read their draft on screen for revision purposes, without needing to actually turn the manuscript pages, make sure your notes are accurately page-referenced.

If you are lucky, and if you have methodically attacked all the problems of your first draft, then the next version may be your last. Sometimes a book may need three or four completely revised drafts before it reaches a final one. Don't despair if this happens—it's quite common. Usually, however, one complete revision is enough, though some fine-tuning might still be needed before you are ready to send it out to a publisher, and you should read it through at least once more with the same critical attention you gave to the first draft.

Objectivity

Objectivity is a very difficult thing for the beginning writer. You have sweated and laboured to produce this book; it is filled with your immortal prose and your best ideas. Now you are expected to pick holes in it, expose its flaws and weaknesses, perhaps perform amputations upon it. It's like being asked to be objective about your own child. But it's worth training yourself to take the necessary one step back from your work. If you don't, other readers certainly will, and much more cruelly than you are capable of.

Sometimes it is helpful at first draft to ask someone else to read it, someone you trust to be honestly critical, but you must steel yourself for their criticisms and be prepared to take them seriously. There has never been a perfect book, certainly no one's first novel, and if yours is ever to hit the marketplace, you will have to accept its imperfections and work at fixing them. The one thing you can be sure of, if you genuinely aspire to be a published writer, is that a professional editor will ask all the hard questions and require you to do whatever work is needed to fix your problems. The need for revision and rewriting doesn't go away when you ignore it, it lurks and festers in the pages of a book that is not as good as it could have been.

Exercises

1. Rewrite a story or chapter of a novel (it needn't be your own), converting it from the third person to the first person, or vice versa. What difference do you notice about such things as characterisation and storyline? Do you like it more or less? Is it successful or not? Why?

2. Write a one-page synopsis of your story or novel, followed by a one-paragraph synopsis, followed by a one-sentence description. If this is too difficult a task, question yourself: If I don't know what my story is about, why should my readers?

11 TAKING CARE OF BUSINESS
Marele Day

How to present your manuscript

You've written your story, it has the potential to be the crime novel of the year. Now it's time for it to leave your writing room and make its way in the world. Contrary to the old cliché, there are cases when a book is judged by its cover. The first impression publishers have of your manuscript is its physical appearance. Presentation is important. Characters in crime novels can be sleazy and down-at-heel, but publishers won't be impressed by a shoddy-looking manuscript. On the other hand, you don't want them to think you're sending a box of chocolates (save that for later).

Your manuscript should look as if it has been written by a professional. Clean, neat copy is easy to read and gives the impression that you are a competent writer. Yours is only one of many manuscripts the publisher has in what is referred to as the 'slush pile'. Good crime novels are fast-paced, they are page turners. If your manuscript is physically difficult to read, e.g. handwritten, full of corrections, dense, with narrow margins, etc., it gives the impression that the story itself is slow and tortuous.

Editing and proofreading are parts of the publishing process but don't send a rough first draft to a publisher on the assumption that the editors will tidy it up. Be sure the novel is as good as you can make it before submitting it. This means paying attention to the structure of your story, its plausibility, the flow of events, checking for any contradictions, and making sure real-life references are accurate (crime fiction fans have a keen eye for detail, so make sure your protagonist is not driving the wrong way down a one-way street). It also means paying attention to the writing itself, to spelling, grammar, punctuation and correcting typographical errors.

Avoid over-designing your manuscript, a temptation if you have computer software that does sophisticated desktop publishing. The writer's job is to write the novel; the publisher will design, package and present that novel as the book that ends up in the shops. Publishers prefer manuscripts not to have the text justified (as it is in a book). It makes typesetting easier if the manuscript is presented with the natural spacing between words.

Some general guidelines for presentation of manuscripts:

title page: title and author's name (upper case, centred on page); copyright line (© writer's name, year); name, address, phone and fax numbers (lower right-hand corner; repeat this info on final page of manuscript)

typing and formatting: professional-looking typeface on white A4 paper (typed on one side of the sheet only) generous margins all round (3–4cm); double or 1.5 spaced. Double spacing allows editors room for comments and makes the manuscript easier to read. Begin each chapter on a new page.

pagination: number pages in top or bottom right-hand corner. Some writers with computers also set up a 'header' or 'footer' which repeats the title of the novel on each page (in case an ill wind blows the pages of your manuscript all over the publisher's office).

binding: loose leaves in a manila folder or wallet-type folder secured with a heavy-duty elastic band or cloth tape.

covering letter: a short accompanying letter that lets the publisher know you're presenting your manuscript for consideration. Mention any literary (or crime!) credentials and previously published work. This could also be the place for dropping a lure that makes the publisher want to read this particular manuscript; a few well-chosen words describing what the novel is about—intriguing without giving too much away. Keep it brief—the less extraneous material publishers have to read the better.

synopsis: a brief summary (one or two pages) of your novel. If a synopsis is required it is worth spending time to make this a document that sells the story to the publisher. There is an art to writing a synopsis, especially for crime novels. Make it succinct, outlining the overall structure of the novel without giving away too many of the plot twists or revealing whodunit and why. That is the pleasure of the text.

floppy disks: in the first instance, submit hard copy only, i.e. the manuscript, but if your submission is successful publishers will usually ask for it on disk (it makes their job easier). So it is wise to make sure that hard-copy text and the text on disk are identical, especially when making final corrections, and that disks are clearly labelled.

Make a phone call to your selected publisher/s to find out the name and position of the person to whom you should send your manuscript—depending on how the company is organised this could be the mass market publisher, the fiction editor etc. Also find out what you should be submitting to that particular publisher. Some publishers initially require a synopsis and a few chapters, others require the whole manuscript.

The normal protocol is to submit your manuscript to one publisher at a time, although increasingly writers are sending copies of their manuscript to several publishers at once. If you are making multiple submissions, let each publisher know. It is essential that you include return postage and a self-addressed envelope large enough to take your manuscript. Don't send your only copy. Publishers take no responsibility for lost manuscripts. Most publishers acknowledge receipt of manuscript. If you haven't had a decision after three months, write a follow-up letter.

Choosing a publisher

Most mainstream companies publish some crime titles. There are also small presses which specialise in crime, such as Wakefield Press, Autopsy and Australian Pocket Press. However, not all publishers have a crime list. It would be a waste of time sending your crime novel to a poetry publisher, or one that specialises in coffee-table books or car manuals. You can cut out a lot of unnecessary heartache, to say nothing of time and money, by first identifying appropriate publishers then sending your work to those most likely to accept it.

How do you do this? Find out who publishes works like yours by browsing in bookshops or libraries. Refer to the Australian Book Publishers Association's *Directory of Members*, which gives names and addresses of publishers in Australia and the kind of material they publish. Send for publishers' catalogues. These provide comprehensive lists of publications from which you can ascertain the kind of novels they are interested in, the 'look' and image they are promoting. Do you like their covers? Do you want to see your book in one of them?

For your interest, here is a list of the contributors to this book and their (crime) publishers in Australia:

Debra Adelaide: McPhee Gribble
Jean Bedford: HarperCollins
Stuart Coupe: Allen & Unwin
J.R. Carroll: Pan Macmillan
Marele Day: Allen & Unwin
Garry Disher: Allen & Unwin
Kerry Greenwood: Penguin
Sandra Harvey: Allen & Unwin, Random Century
Stephen Knight: Allen & Unwin
Nigel Krauth: Allen & Unwin
Robert Wallace: HarperCollins
Minette Walters: Allen & Unwin

Overseas publication is difficult to negotiate long-distance and usually requires an agent, particularly in the US. You can familiarise yourself with overseas markets by consulting reference books such as *Writers' and Artists' Yearbook* or R.R. Bowker's *Literary Market Place*, which provide details about book and magazine publishers throughout the world, and information about agents and their requirements, awards and prizes, writers' groups and organisations. These publications can be found in state and some local libraries.

Agents

Agents don't take on material unless they think it has publishing potential. While publishers read at least part of every manuscript sent to them, they take submissions from agents more seriously because they feel such manuscripts have already passed one screening process. Publishers are likely to give agents greater feedback and more specific reasons why, for example, they might be rejecting a manuscript.

If a manuscript is accepted, the agent will try to negotiate the best deal for the client. Some agents draw up their own contract on behalf of the writer and present this to the publisher. They negotiate on your behalf for better royalties and contractual terms, and may have input into the kind of promotion your book will receive. They can also seek markets for, and negotiate the sale of, subsidiary rights such as film, television and radio, translation, large print/talking book, rights to print extracts, abridgements and condensations.

Agents often suggest suitable authors for anthologies and other publishing projects, and find their clients work as guest speakers at literary festivals, on panels and in schools.

Agents take a percentage (10–20 per cent) of your earnings and some charge a fee to read your manuscript in the first place. Deciding whether or not to have an agent is a matter of personal choice. Some writers never have one, some begin with an agent. Others engage one when they feel their career needs managing. An agent is essential for scriptwriters, but many book writers deal directly with their publisher.

An agent would be useful in the following circumstances:

- You have a publishable manuscript but have difficulty accessing the market because, for example, you live in a remote area; rather than researching the markets yourself you would prefer to place your manuscript with someone who is in constant contact with publishers and knows this market well.
- You feel a third person would be better able to speak on your behalf. Saying 'This is the crime novel of the decade and you must publish it' sounds more convincing coming from someone other than the author.
- You feel you don't have enough experience and legal expertise to negotiate the most favourable contract yourself.

If you're considering getting an agent, do some research. Ask other writers or appropriate people in the industry about agents. Is a particular agent reliable? What kind of reputation does he or she have? Find out which agents represent crime writers. Consult D.W. Thorpe's *Who's Who of Australian Writers*. Where a particular writer has an agent, the agent's name is listed.

Approaching an agent

You approach an agent in much the same way you would approach a publisher, either by sending material directly or by making a phone call. An initial phone call to an agent serves several purposes. It:

- establishes a personal contact between you and the agency
- makes your name familiar to them
- determines what your next step will be.

Sometimes a secretary or assistant will handle the call. They might tell you to write to the agency saying that you are interested in being represented by it, with a brief outline of your work and a résumé. As with publishers, not all agents require the same things. One agent might request the finished manuscript while another will want a synopsis and sample chapters.

Often agents will speak to you directly. This helps them ascertain who you are, what your novel is about, what stage you're at in your writing development and whether they can help you. If they are busy, or not taking new clients, they may suggest a suitable publisher or another avenue you could explore.

A selection of agents who handle fiction:

The Almost Managing Company
PO Box 1034
Carlton Vic 3053
ph: (03) 9347 1800 fax: (03) 9347 0235

Anthony Williams Management
1st floor, 50 Oxford St
Paddington NSW 2021
ph: (02) 360 3833 fax: (02) 360 3189

Australian Literary Management
2 Buckland St
Chippendale NSW 2008
ph: (02) 211 0252 fax: (02) 212 2350
or
2a Armstrong St
Middle Park Vic 3206
ph: (03) 9690 8173 fax: (03) 9690 2598

The Cameron Creswell Agency
Suite 5, Edgecliff Court
2 New McLean St
Edgecliff NSW 2027
ph: (02) 362 0600 fax: (02) 363 3317

Margaret Connolly
37 Ormond St
Paddington NSW 2021
ph: (02) 331 6578 fax: (02) 331 3875

Curtis Brown (Aust)
23 Union St
Paddington NSW 2021
ph: (02) 361 6161 (02) 331 5301 fax: (02) 360 3935

Golvan Arts Management
PO Box 766
Kew Vic 3101
ph: (03) 9853 5341 fax: (03) 9853 8555

Hickson Associates
PO Box 271
Woollahra NSW 2025
ph: (02) 362 3303 fax: (02) 362 3629

Rejection and what to do about it

More than 15 000 unsolicited manuscripts are presented annually to publishers in Australia. Penguin alone receives over 5000 of these but publishes only four or five new writers in a year. So, statistically, chances of publication are slim and you'll be in the overwhelming majority if you receive a rejection. Sometimes a rejection slip will indicate why the manuscript was rejected but more often than not it will be a simple 'This is not for us.'

If you have done your homework and sent your book to an appropriate publisher 'this is not for us' could mean that the publisher has a quota of similiar novels in the pipeline. If you keep getting rejections, it may be that the manuscript is not individual enough or of a publishable standard. What can you do about it?

Writing is a solitary activity but it is often difficult for the writer alone to see what needs to be done to bring the manuscript to a publishable standard. You may need to let this one go, consider it a trial run, and get on with the next story. If you feel that your work has potential but you need advice about rewriting and editing, there are several avenues available to you.

For a fee, you can have the manuscript professionally assessed. An assessment is a written report (usually a couple of pages) which signals the strengths and weaknesses of your work and provides suggestions for rewriting and editing. The National Book Council has a manuscript assessment service, as do the Australian Society of Authors and some of the state Writers' Centres. The assessors are usually experienced writers or editors. The Society of Editors also has members who do freelance assessments for writers.

Join a writers' organisation such as the Australian Society of Authors or the Fellowship of Australian Writers. These have meetings and workshops where you can present excerpts from your work and get feedback on it. Writers' Centres in various states also have workshops and seminars which will be helpful. Membership of writers' organisations gives you a sense of community with other writers, and their newsletters disseminate information relevant to writers and keep you informed of workshops, competitions, prizes etc.

Adult and community education organisations have a variety of creative writing classes taught by published writers.

The process of publishing

If it is your happy fate to be accepted for publication your novel will go along the conveyor belt that turns manuscripts into finished books. Once you have submitted your manuscript, it is read by a professional reader (either in-house or freelance). The reader considers the novel, assessing its strengths and weaknesses, marketability and publishability. If the publisher or commissioning editor accepts the reader's recommendation to publish, the manuscript is discussed with the sales and marketing department, the managing director, and designers. They make decisions about it regarding marketing strategies, number of copies in the first print run, and the recommended retail price.

On acceptance of your manuscript, you will be sent a contract. This sets out the conditions and terms of publication, including the royalty rate. This is usually 10 per cent of the recommended retail price. An average first print run in Australia is 3000 books. So if the book retails for $12.95 and the print run sells out, you will receive $3885, a far cry from the fabled sums that make headline news. A proportion of this money will be paid to you as an advance on royalties, usually half on signing the contract and the other half on delivery of manuscript or publication day. Your book will have to sell enough copies to cover the advance before any further royalties are paid to you.

While you will no doubt be overjoyed to hear that the publisher has accepted your novel (in fact, if your manuscript has been rejected a few times already you might feel like paying them!), don't lose sight of the fact that the contract is a business arrangement and a legally binding document. Read it carefully and make sure you understand what you are signing. If you have an agent they will go through the contract with you. Otherwise, it is a good idea to have someone with legal expertise interpret it for you. Writers' organisations such as the Australian Society of Authors and other organisations such as the Arts Law Centre of Australia and the Australian Copyright Council may also be of assistance.

Once the contract is signed, your manuscript will pass along the production line. First step is editing. The editor, as well as attending to grammatical details, typographical errors etc., can suggest structural changes. She is looking at your manuscript as an enlightened reader. Her job is to make the manuscript as good as it can possibly get. Don't be put off by the number of notes and 'corrections' all over your once-pristine manuscript. It's not a school essay and anyway, you've already passed. The editor is on your side. It is better that suggestions come in time to make changes rather than have critics point these things out after the book is published. You may not agree with everything the editor says. Try to view your work objectively. If after consideration you still disagree, discuss the matter with the editor. In the end, you are the author of the work.

The next step in the process is designing the book. This involves making decisions about format, typeface and cover design. You will be consulted to a large or small extent on these matters, depending on the publisher.

Once page proofs (unbound typeset pages of the book) are available, they are read by both a professional proofreader and the author. It is now several months since you have submitted your manuscript and with a fresher eye you will probably get the urge to change things. Unless there is a glaring oversight, resist this urge. Apart from correcting type-setting errors, changes to the text at this stage cost money. Rewriting and editing should have been satisfactorily completed long before the page-proof stage.

Now you sit back and wait until publication day. Media releases and review copies of the book will be sent out. If you are the next John Grisham or P.D. James, publication will be surrounded by a huge promotion campaign. You will tour internationally, be feted, and say how exhausting it is and that you'd rather be home writing. Whether you sell 200 000 copies or 2000, though, the true reward is knowing that the story you laboured over in solitary confinement is now out there in the real world. You will have the pleasure of seeing your book in the bookstores and people you don't even know avidly reading it on the train.

Crime writers' organisations

In Australia
The Australian Crime Writers' Association was formed in late 1995 over a boozy lunch. With membership open to writers and fans, it aims to promote Australian crime fiction through the annual Ned Kelly Award for Best Crime Fiction.

Contact: Peter Milne
Abbey's Bookshop
131 York Street
Sydney NSW 2000.

According to its brochure, **Sisters in Crime** is 'Australia's fastest growing literary society and, arguably, also its fastest growing women's organisation.' Originally founded in the US by Sara Paretsky and others to promote women's crime writing, its membership is made up of writers, publishers, booksellers and readers (of both sexes) who enjoy crime fiction by women. It has a newsletter, arranges meetings and functions, and administers an annual short story competition, the Scarlet Stiletto Award.

Sisters in Crime
GPO Box 5319 BB
Melbourne, Vic 3001
inquiries for new members: Helen Halliday (03) 9525 3852

Contacts in other states:

Queensland: Mysteries & Movies Bookshop (07) 844 0688
New South Wales: Margaret Carew-Reid (02) 334 4355
South Australia: Jenny Weight (08) 377 1157
Western Australia: Val Marsden (09) 272 4203
Australian Capital Territory: Caitlin O'Connor (06) 282 5173

Overseas

The **International Association of Crime Writers** is 'an organisation of professional writers whose primary goals are to promote communication among writers of all nationalities, to encourage translation of crime fiction and nonfiction into other languages, and to speak out against censorship and other forms of tyranny.' There are branches worldwide (except in Australia). Contact:

K. Arne Blom, President
Smaskolevagen 22
S-224-67 Lund
Sweden

In the US there is a proliferation of crime writers' organisations, some of which have international membership. The better known among these are:

American Crime Writers League
Jay Brandon
219 Tuxedo
San Antonio
TX 78209
USA
(published writers only)

Mystery Writers of America
Priscilla Ridgeway, Executive Director
6th floor, 17 E. 47th St
New York
NY 10017
USA
(published writers and some publishing professionals)

Private Eye Writers of America
Robert Randisi, Executive Director
4239—H Barcelos Dr.
St Louis
MO 63129
USA
(writers, fans and publishing professionals)

Sisters in Crime
Box 442124
Lawrence
KS 66044-8933
USA
(writers and fans)

In Britain the principal organisation is:

Crime Writers' Association
Anthea Fraser, Secretary
'Owlswick'
22 Chiltern Way
Tring
Herts HP23 5JK
UK
(published writers of crime fiction and nonfiction; associate membership for agents, publishers, reviewers of crime fiction)

Publications

Australia's crime and mystery magazine, **Mean Streets**, has an international focus with a leaning towards the hardboiled.

Informative and chatty, it contains articles and reviews of contemporary writers as well as offbeat pieces on noir classics.

Mean Streets
ed. Stuart Coupe and Julie Ogden
214 Hat Hill Road
Blackheath NSW 2785

The Armchair Detective Book of Lists (ed. Kate Stine, Otto Penzler Books, New York, 1995) is 'the definitive source for all the essential and entertaining lists every mystery writer, collector and fan *must* have'. It contains complete listings of major crime awards and their winners, critics' and authors' favourite crime books, etc, and has information on (mainly American) mystery organisations, fan clubs, conventions and publications.

Specialist bookshops

Gaslight Books
First Floor, Bonner Court
Neptune Street
Woden ACT 2609

Kill City
126 Greville St
Prahran Vic 3181

Abbey's Bookshop
131 York Street
Sydney NSW 2000

Browsing on Browning
11 Browning Street
South Brisbane Qld 4101

Internet

Welcome to the 21st century. The Mysterious Homepage, operated from Denmark by Jan B. Steffensen, is the definitive starting point for Internet crime buffs. It provides listings of mystery resources such as magazines and CDROMS, as well as links to a plethora of mystery sites.

Its address is:
http://www.db.dk/dbaa/jbs/homepage.htm

12 THE READER'S POINT OF VIEW

Stuart Coupe

Why me?

There are moments when I imagine what my epitaph might be. When the time comes I'll be planted six feet under, surrounded by massive piles of unread manuscripts that people are still hoping I'll get to read—even if it happens to be in the afterlife.

My tombstone will be inscribed with the words: 'Here lies Stuart Coupe, who read more unsolicited Australian crime fiction than anyone else. It was a dirty job, but someone had to do it.' Sounds nice, doesn't it? Chisel it on a slab of marble painted blood red. Blast it with a few bullets fired at point-blank range. No flowers, thanks, just a few knives protruding out of the dirt.

Why me? That's a question I've asked myself frequently over the past five years, every time the postman has arrived with another five unsolicited manuscripts. Hey, some people have even sent me completed novels and seem less than impressed when I return the 400 or so double-spaced pages and gently explain that *Mean Streets* is a magazine and as such doesn't publish novels ('The first 300 pages are great. Don't suppose you could prune it down to 15, could you?').

The main reason that so many manuscripts have been foisted on yours truly is that before *Mean Streets* was launched in late 1990 there were very few outlets for crime fiction in Australia. There was a monthly crime story competition run in conjunction with an airline, the best stories being published in its in-flight magazine and subsequently in a couple of Golden Dagger Awards anthologies. Every so often a popular magazine or newspaper would publish a new crime or mystery story, although usually they were written by established writers like Peter Corris or Jennifer Rowe.

Along came *Mean Streets* and suddenly every would-be-Corris or Rowe started deluging me with stories. I'm a magazine editor, I expect to be sent material, but I couldn't believe the amount of crime that was being written out there. Let's do some simple mathematics: an average of five stories a week over five years adds up to more than 1250 pieces of short crime fiction. As I write this I'm surrounded by piles of manuscripts, some that were sent two years ago. I keep trying to remind writers that, at best, *Mean Streets* comes out four times a year and that there are never more than two fiction pieces in each issue. How many times have I written to writers saying that I really like their story but the earliest I could possibly look at publishing it is in the second issue in 2001?

These days I'm just not reading new manuscripts. I simply don't have time and the initial enthusiasm has, sadly, worn off. In the early days of *Mean Streets* I was genuinely excited by the thought that hidden amidst the huge piles of paper were one or two truly astonishing new, undiscovered Australian crime fiction writers. I read, and I read, and I read—and I read. With one or two minor exceptions I was always disappointed.

Some days I simply got angry. There was the time I read a twenty-page story about fishing. I kept turning the pages thinking that some element of crime must enter the story soon. Having finished, I wondered whether I was stupid and had simply failed to notice that the writer meant the interaction between the fisherman and his prey to be some sort of metaphor for crime in our times. Maybe the guy with the fishing rod was meant to symbolise the serial killer in society, randomly picking victims from the innocents swimming in the great pond of life. Eventually I decided it was nothing more or less than a fishing story.

I wrote back to the author suggesting that the story might be better suited to *Fishing News*—and that maybe he'd like to send me the crime story he'd obviously mistakenly sent to them.

But that's digressing into the area of knowing your market and checking out publications before submitting fiction to them. The fact is that almost all of the unsolicited crime and mystery fiction I've read over the years has been unpublishable. That's not to denigrate the efforts of the writers who tried their hardest, but these stories had serious flaws: unbelievable, unrealistic, stilted dialogue; plots that just didn't make sense; truly ridiculous coincidences that led to the denouement; characters that were like cardboard cut-outs, and so forth. Obviously, the writers didn't have access to a book like this.

Make no mistake, writing a successful crime story or novel is hard work. Crime has traditionally been regarded as a second-class genre and this leads many people to think that it's an easy one to work in. They should think again. That assumption is the primary reason that for every memorable story or novel published there are a couple of hundred that should have stayed hidden under the author's bed. Writing so-called 'genre' fiction is every bit as difficult as writing anything else. In fact, after reading far too many examples of 'the great novel of self-indulgence', I can't help but wish that more writers were forced to adhere to the rigid disciplines of crime fiction.

Yes, Virginia, there are rules

Virtually all of the authors who sent stories to *Mean Streets* ignored, or were unaware of, some of the golden rules for writing crime, mystery and detective fiction. Back in 1982 I stumbled on a book called the *Mystery Writers Handbook*, compiled by the Mystery Writers of America. It contained a terrific preface by editor Lawrence Treat, who pointed to four (just four) essential elements of this type of writing. I'm going to quote Treat in full because I've never since read anything so succinct about the craft of writing a really compelling short story or novel.

Rule 1: There must be a crime and it must be personalised to the point where the reader cares. Usually, but not always, the crime is a murder, since murder is the most serious crime known to man. The readers must want to see its solution, must want to see the criminal caught. If a troop of cowboys shoots up a town and happens to wing the town drunk, nobody cares particularly whether the marauders are caught. But if the shooting is intentional and the town drunk turns out to be a spy in disguise, or if the murderer is the unknown bandit with a pair of toucan bills in his hat, then the reader's interest is aroused and he longs to see justice done and the mystery solved.

Rule 2: The criminal must appear reasonably early in the story. Although one of the jobs of the author is to conceal the identity of the murderer from the readers, this does not give the author a license to introduce a totally new character on page 214 and reveal him as the murderer on page 215. The villain of the piece must be evident for a goodly portion of the book.

Rule 3: The author must be rigorously honest, and all clues, whether physical, such as a fingerprint or a dropped purple bandanna, a character trait, or an emotional relationship between people, must be made available to the reader. He is the alter ego of the protagonist and the reader must know everything that the protagonist knows. Under no circumstances, for example, can Mr Detective point to Mr Killer and say, 'You are the guilty party because you are left-handed,' unless somewhere in the story (cleverly concealed, of course) it has been established that only a left-handed person could have killed Mr Victim, and that Mr Killer, and no one else, is left-handed. In a similar manner, the dithery schoolteacher cannot be disclosed at the end of the story as the vicious spy unless somewhere along the line she's been revealed as a former actress or she shows herself capable of vicious, non-dithery behaviour.

Rule 4: The detective must exert effort to catch the criminal, and the criminal must exert effort to fool the detective and escape from him. Coincidence is taboo. Sherlock Bones can't sit and think in his Leatherette armchair, while Moriarty holes up in comfort, until a passer-by happens to notify Sherlock that there's a funny-looking guy down the street. Whereupon Sherlock stops thinking, Moriarty stops holing up, and Sherlock nabs Moriarty and then explains that he really expected this to happen all the time.

Simple rules? Sure, but it's surprising how often at least one (and usually all four) is ignored and the reader is left with a totally unsatisfying story. And let's face it—there's nothing more frustrating than reading three-quarters of a short story or novel, loving every page, and then having the entire experience ruined by some totally stooopid conclusion.

One example of this that sticks in my mind is a novel written by a well-known Australian author a few years back. I still believe the book is a superior piece of crime fiction, but when I arrived at the final twenty pages I was ready to hurl the damn thing at the wall—or the author, if he'd been in hitting distance. You see, for over 300 pages a secondary character was the picture of sweetness and light. Supportive, friendly, up front, etc. Then, completely out of the blue, he turned into a complete and utter bastard and it was 'revealed' that all along he had been the figure of evil behind all the mayhem. This is just not on.

I forgave the author—but only just—because the novel was so suspenseful and peopled with such wonderfully drawn characters that the trip to the last twenty pages had been marvellous. But the conclusion stopped the book from being the truly great piece of crime fiction it had the potential to be.

Grab 'em, hold 'em and don't let go till you're finished

There's a game I often play with crime-fiction-loving guests, and it provides an interesting insight into what can attract a reader to a book. When I started working as a journalist, the most valuable lesson learned was from a gnarled old journo who came up to my desk one day and said, 'Always remember, if you don't hook them with the first paragraph then there's no chance they'll read the others.'

In this game, we take turns reading the opening paragraphs of crime novels. The idea is for the other participants to identify both the writer and the book and then say whether they'd want to buy and read the book after skimming that paragraph in a shop.

There are three opening paragraphs that I've re-read dozens of times over the years as perfect openings. One's from a short story, the other two from novels:

> There was a desert wind blowing that night. It was one of those hot dry Santa Anas that come down through the mountain passes and curl your hair and make your nerves jump and your skin itch. On nights like that every booze party ends in a fight. Meek little wives feel the edge of the carving knife and study their husbands' necks. Anything can happen. You can even get a full glass of beer at a cocktail lounge.
>
> Raymond Chandler, 'Red Wind' (1946)

> The pretender to the Emperor's throne was a fat thirty-seven-year-old Chinaman called Artie Wu who always jogged along Malibu Beach right after dawn even in summer, when dawn came round as early as 4:42. It was while jogging along the beach just east of the Paradise Cove pier that he tripped over a dead pelican, fell, and met the man with six greyhounds. It was the sixteenth of June, a Thursday.
>
> Ross Thomas, *Chinaman's Chance* (1978)

> When I finally caught up with Abraham Trahearne, he was drinking beer with an alcoholic bulldog named Fireball Roberts in a ramshackle joint just outside of Sonoma, California, drinking the heart right out of a fine spring afternoon.
>
> James Crumley, *The Last Good Kiss* (1978)

After openings like that, you know you're in the hands of a superlative writer, regardless of what genre they write in. In my humble opinion they sure beat the hell out of openings like 'There was a body in the library. Mrs James would never play bridge again. The butler was nowhere to be seen.' Hm, actually that's not too bad!

Plotted or (almost) plotless?

Much is made in the media of the myriad of subgenres operating under the banner of crime fiction. Books are increasingly categorised and sub-subcategorised. It's no longer good enough to write a crime story—people want to put it in a pigeonhole like private eye, medical thriller, courtroom drama, hardboiled (crikey, there are even medium and softboiled categories in some magazines), police procedural, clue puzzle, dark mystery.

I've become more partial to another category: plotless. I consider the attachment to plot or the lack of it the most important dividing line between readers of crime fiction.

There is a school of readers whose primary interest in devouring a crime novel is the complexity of the plot and entering into a brain battle with the author to see if they can unravel the mystery before the end of the book. Oh, the smug looks I've seen over the years: 'It was so obvious that Aunt Mavis had done it. You could tell by page 76 that no one else could possibly have killed Mildred.' Such readers expect all of Treat's four rules to be adhered to. For them, the mystery is everything. Nothing is more important than the plot.

Personally, I rarely give a damn about plots. It's nice to have some semblance of one, but a semblance is all it needs to be. I'd say that with a good two-thirds of my favourite books I have only the vaguest idea of what's been going on. Frequently I'll challenge friends by saying, 'Look, I dare you— explain to me the plot of one, just one Raymond Chandler novel. It's obvious Chandler had no idea, so how can you expect to?'

I read the books of James Ellroy, unquestionably the finest writer dealing with themes of criminality in the past decade, with a notebook by my side to help give me a vague idea of the characters and plot. It's usually a fruitless task and after 100 pages I realise I'm attempting the impossible.

So why do I read books when for the most part I don't have a real grasp of what's going on? I read them for the dialogue, characterisation, sense of place and, in the best instances, the sheer poetry of the writing. That doesn't mean you can do away with the plot altogether. We're talking about the greats here, and though their plots may resemble scrambled eggs, there is still something driving the story along. A while back I was interviewing the aging rock 'n' roll legend Lou Reed. We were chatting about our shared passion for contemporary American crime fiction. At one point the name James Lee Burke, who writes inspired novels featuring sometimes, sometimes-not cop Dave Robicheaux, came up. Reed had recently read Burke's novel *Black Cherry Blues*. 'He's just not a crime writer, man,' he drawled. 'James Lee Burke is a poet.'

In his masterpiece, *Heaven's Prisoners*, Burke delivers one killer insight after another. Take this:

> I thought about my father and wished he were there with me. He couldn't read or write and never once travelled outside the state of Louisiana, but his heart possessed an intuitive understanding about our lives, our Cajun vision of the world, that no philosophy book could convey. He drank too much and he'd fistfight two or three men in a bar at the same time, with the enthusiasm of a boy hitting baseballs; but inside he had a gentle heart, a strong sense of right and wrong, and a tragic sense about the cruelty and violence that the world sometimes imposes upon the innocent.

Or this:

> Most people think of violence as an abstraction. It never is. It's always ugly, it always demeans and dehumanises, it always shocks and repels and leaves the witnesses to it sick and shaken. It's meant to do all these things.

Aside from his breathtaking insights and characterisation, Burke is a masterful re-creator of time and place. I've never been to New Iberia in Louisiana but I know it as well as any place I've visited. I know the smell of the rain, the roads, the appearance of the trees, the best place to eat, and the vernacular of its inhabitants.

The same goes for the majority of my other favourite writers. Even though I've travelled to New York more than a dozen times, I've never seen the city that Andrew Vachss and Lawrence Block conjure up and describe. I know Texas through the writing of Joe R. Lansdale, Montana through James Crumley, Chicago through Eugene Izzi and Los Angeles through Robert Campbell, Walter Mosley and James Ellroy, its best chroniclers since the days of Raymond Chandler.

My perception of Sydney is intertwined with that of Peter Corris in his Cliff Hardy novels, books that Bob Hudson once described as being like 'listening to Abe Saffron read the *Gregory's*.' Gabrielle Lord's *Whipping Boy*, Marele Day's (hey, I'll do anything to crawl to an editor) *The Life and Crimes of Harry Lavender* contain equally evocative portraits of Sydney, and J.R. Carroll and Garry Disher obviously have the grittiness of the mean streets of Melbourne under their fingertips and smeared all over their boots. Melbourne, you're walking in it . . . hmmm, not a bad line.

Yes—place, character, vernacular and insight. They're my four essential ingredients for elevating an ordinary crime caper into something unforgettable.

Let me throw another example at you. This one's from Lawrence Block's *A Dance at the Slaughterhouse*:

Afterwards I went back to the hotel. No messages. I sat in my room reading for two hours. Someone had passed along a paperback volume called *The Newgate Calendar*, a case-by-case report on British crimes of the seventeenth and eighteenth centuries. I'd had it around for a month or so, and at night I would read a few pages before I went to sleep. It was mostly interesting, although some cases were more interesting than others. What got me some nights, though, was the way nothing changed. People back then killed each other for every reason and no reason, and they did it with every means at their disposal and all the ingenuity they could bring to bear. Sometimes it provided a good antidote for the morning paper, with its deadlily daily chronicle of contemporary crime. It was easy to read the paper every day and conclude that humanity was infinitely worse than ever, that the world was going to hell and that hell was where we belonged. Then, when I read about men and women killing each other centuries ago for pennies or for love, I could tell myself that we weren't getting worse after all, that we were as good as we'd ever been. On other nights that same revelation brought not reassurance but despair. We had been ever thus. We were not getting better, we would never get better. Anyone along the way who'd died for our sins had died for nothing. We had more sins in reserve, we had a supply that would last for all eternity.

Now, after reading that, can you blame anyone for reading *A Dance at the Slaughterhouse* for reasons other than just wanting to find out if weather-beaten private eye, Matthew Scudder, solves the case?

Realistically that's unrealistic

My journey through crime and mystery fiction began as a kid reading Enid Blyton's Famous Five and Secret Seven books. It progressed to devouring all of my grandmother's Agatha Christie books—and she had a *lot* of them. The first one I read was *The Mysterious Affair at Styles* and my favourite remains *The Murder of Roger Ackroyd*. Some years later, at university I discovered the world of the private eye in books by Dashiell Hammett, Raymond Chandler, Ross Macdonald, and John D. MacDonald with his non-private eye character Travis McGee. A year or two later the so-called renaissance of Australian crime fiction began with the appearance of *The Dying Trade*, Peter Corris's first Cliff Hardy yarn. I was an instant convert, not being alone in warming to a protagonist whose vernacular, locale, and personality were far more familiar than those of his overseas counterparts.

For many years just about all I read was private eye fiction. I was enamoured of the weather-beaten, hard-drinkin', trench-coated private eye in his seedy office, slugging on a bottle of scotch and just managing to save the (always) blonde dame in distress, getting beaten up so many times along the way that it was surprising he could tell the difference between a lamp post and the dame.

These days there's only a handful of private eye books I can read without wincing. The biggest problem is that the traditional stereotype has become outmoded and unrealistic. As someone joked recently, 'When was the last time a real-life private eye investigated a murder? The last time was never.'

Times have changed and aside from not being involved with murders (or divorces for that matter), the private eye of the '90s is a vastly different beast from his counterpart in the '40s and '50s. For starters, as is reflected in contemporary fiction, he may not be a bloke. I don't need to tell anyone reading this about the rise of women crime writers, particularly those with private eyes as protagonists, over the past decade.

But, as any working private eye will tell you, treading the mean streets is absolutely the last resort in their line of work. In an early issue of *Mean Streets* I ran an article by Jerry Kennealy, who is not only an accomplished writer of crime fiction but a licensed and practising private investigator. In it he points out countless differences between the reality of being a private investigator and the mythology of fiction. A crucial example is that 'the fictional chap doesn't use a computer nearly enough. The real private eye's best friend isn't his trench coat, his .45 or the bottle of bourbon in the bottom drawer of his desk. It's his computer. And his printer and his fax machine. You cannot exist in the business without them.'

Being accurate about the methods of investigation is, I believe, important. One *Mean Streets* reader is on a crusade to expose crime writers who haven't done their homework in matters pertaining to firearms. He is forever writing to me listing novels in which a character snicks off the safety catch of a revolver. As he always tells me, revolvers don't have safety catches. There are so many books on forensic science, weapons, poisons and so forth around these days that it's hard to think that writers who make mistakes like that are being anything but extremely lazy in their research habits.

Crime, and particularly private eye, fiction is changing. I'm starting to see letters in overseas publications from private eye writers, particularly blokes, whining about how no-one wants to know about their (almost certainly stereotyped) private eye novel. Aside from the courtroom saga (thank you Scott Turow, John Grisham and your dozens of imitators), the two perennially popular, and realistic, subgenres of crime fiction are the (practising or renegade) police procedural and the innocent-in-trouble novel.

Let's face it, cops are always going to be the ones investigating murders and serious crime, and the myriad of characters found in any division of the police force gives the writer an enormous array of material while still keeping the action within realistic bounds. And some of the most memorable characters in recent crime fiction have been those renegade outsiders who've either left the force or are still there and struggling to come to terms with their day jobs.

The innocent-in-trouble scenario is, I believe, one of the most effective and realistic—and a sure way to draw in readers like me. Who hasn't wondered about being caught up in random acts of violence, being in the wrong place at the wrong time, or opening the door late at night and finding your worst nightmare waiting outside? Possibly this partly accounts for the popularity of the serial killer novel in recent years, as thousands of readers are viscerally drawn to reading about hideous events that could happen any time, anywhere. Possibly readers gain perverse reassurance from such books because after the human carnage justice is usually done, good triumphs over evil, and order is reinstated.

Far more frightening and, unfortunately, more realistic are the increasing number of crime novels in which the white knight does not win the day and the perpetrators live to kill again. Certainly such an outcome is seen in a minority of books, but in this day and age it's regrettably a very realistic one.

To kill or not to kill the series character

Oh, the quandary of the series character-creating crime writer. You've had a few successful books featuring heroes with such unlikely names as Cliff Hardy, Phryne Fisher, Verity Birdwood, Claudia Valentine, Wyatt (yep, just Wyatt), Syd Fish and Scobie Malone. The readers love 'em. They hang out for each instalment to see whether Cliff's on or off the booze, or who Claudia's invited home this time. They begin to feel like they're yapping over the fence with a friendly neighbour: 'Oh, Mavis, you won't believe this but that gruff Mr Hardy down the road drove home in a new Falcon this afternoon. I swear it's a '65 model,' or 'Syd, I must tell you, that young Claudia has no taste. I saw her come back to the pub last night with this *thing*—it could have been a walking corpse for all I know. Look, there's blokes like us, we may be getting on a bit . . . yeah, I know your 80th's coming up in a few weeks . . .but *puhleez.'*

And it's not just readers who become drawn to the personality of a series character. Publishers love 'em too. It's called a backlist. If one of the books sells big time, you can just see their eyes glinting: 'Bob, a new advertising campaign . . . "if you loved *M is for Moron*, you'll delight in *B is for Boring, C is for Cat* and all the others in Sam Grumpy's acclaimed series, winner of the 1995 Wet Trenchcoat Award." '

Readers often discover such books midway through a series and are attracted to earlier ones largely because they like the main character. By the same token, once they've become close to Cliff, Phyrne, Claudia *et al.* they hang out for the next instalment.

Series characters in crime fiction, however, have at least two drawbacks—they tend to be unrealistic, and it's hard to get rid of them. How many cops or private eyes score virtually *all* of the truly interesting, mind-bogglingly fascinating cases in their town? Gee whiz, most of them spend so much time tramping the mean streets that even if they had to do any paperwork (you know, like reports), they'd never have time. No sooner have they captured the brutal psychopath who's killed 75 people in the last fortnight than the phone rings. Another body. Another killer. Let's go.

And talking of realism, would anyone like to inspect the brain and body of most series characters after the physical punishment they are subjected to over the course of several novels? A reviewer once counted how many times Cliff Hardy was beaten unconscious in one book, OK, it *was* a collection of short stories but the Hardster lost consciousness some 24 times in fewer than 200 pages. After that sort of treatment (and let's not forget there are almost 20 Hardy books), it's a minor miracle Cliff can still write his name, let alone work out how to put the key in the Falcon's ignition. But can you imagine a Hardy novel without a serious bit of biffo being directed at Cliff? OK, OK, I hear you scream—the crime novel is meant to be entertaining. No argument there, but for me, to *just* be entertaining just ain't enough.

Equally problematic for the writer is getting sick of the series character. A reader can just stop buying the damn books, but it's more difficult for the writer if he or she gets to the point where they can't stand the sight of their chief protagonist. Can you imagine Sue Grafton's publishers issuing a press release saying 'the alphabet stops at M'? Ain't gonna happen.

In reality most series characters should be dead after three or four books. The law of averages says that they're going to cop serious (read dead) bullet damage at some point in the course of those books. Oh, sure: 'Fifteen bullets missed my heart by half a centimetre and my trusty offsider just happened to burst through the door at exactly the right time on 16 occasions.' Gimme a break. It's fine for Batman and Robin—or Superman, for that matter—but in the real world that's just not the way things work.

A lot of crime writers start other series or write non-series books to temporarily escape these dilemmas, but in almost every case it's the series character that they're best known for. Still, if you want my opinion, which you're getting anyway, kill 'em all.

But on a more serious (gulp) note, it's important for writers to weigh up the pros and cons of series characters. I probably don't need to remind you that many of the most successful writers are in that position because of their series characters— so they must have *something* going for them.

Of course there are countless writers of crime fiction who have an extremely consistent style and thematic content but decide not to use the same central character in each book—

and others who just have minor characters reappear from time to time in cameo roles. The choice is always yours. And let's not forget that if you get tired of a series character there's nothing to stop you having him terminated in the manner of your choice. What a great title for your first novel—*Who Is Killing the Great Series Characters of Crime?* There's a good yarn there somewhere. See you on the bookstands.

Bibliography

Bacia, Jennifer, *Creating Popular Fiction*, Allen & Unwin, Sydney, 1994

Barrett, Robert, *White Shoes, White Lines and Blackie*, Pan Macmillan, Sydney, 1992

Bendel, Stephanie Kay, *Making Crime Pay: A Practical Guide to Mystery Writing*, Prentice-Hall, New York, 1983

Bintliff, Russell, *Police Procedural: A Writer's Guide to the Police and How They Work* Writer's Digest, Cincinnati, 1993

Block, Lawrence, *Telling Lies for Fun and Profit*, Arbor House, New York, 1981

Blythe, Hal, C. Sweet & J. Landreth, *Private Eyes: A Writer's Guide to Private Investigators*, Writer's Digest Books, Cincinnati, 1993

Campbell, Ross, 'Ross Campbell' in *Self Portraits* ed. David Foster, National Library of Australia, Canberra, 1991

Cawelti, John, *Adventure, Mystery and Romance: Formula Stories as Art and Popular Culture*, University of Chicago Press, 1976

Chandler, Raymond (eds. D. Gardiner and K.S. Walker), *Raymond Chandler Speaking*, Hamilton, London, 1962

Conrad, Barnaby, *The Complete Guide to Writing Fiction*, Writer's Digest Books, Cincinnati, 1990

Cooper-Clark, D., *Designs of Darkness: Interviews with Detective Novelists*, 1983

Corris, Peter, *White Meat*, Pan Macmillan, Sydney, 1981

Day, Marele, *The Life and Crimes of Harry Lavender*, Allen & Unwin, Sydney, 1987

—— *The Last Tango of Dolores Delgado*, Allen & Unwin, Sydney, 1992

Doubtfire, Dianne, *The Craft of Novel Writing*, Allison & Busby, London & New York, 1978

Epel, Naomi, *Writers Dreaming*, Carol Sothern Books, New York, 1993

Field, Syd, *Screenplay: The Foundations of Screenwriting*, Delta, 1979

—— *The Screenwriter's Workbook*, Dell Publishing, 1984

Friedman, Kinky, *Frequent Flyer*, Morrow, New York, 1989

Grafton, Sue (ed.), *Writing Mysteries: A Handbook by the Mystery Writers of America*, Writer's Digest Books, Cincinnati, 1993

Highsmith, Patricia, *Plotting and Writing Suspense Fiction*, Poplar Press, London, 1983

Keating, H.R.F. *Writing Crime Fiction*, St Martin's Press, New York, 1987

Klauser, H.A., *Writing on Both Sides of the Brain*, Harper & Row, San Francisco, 1986

Koontz, Dean, *How to Write Best-Selling Fiction*, Writer's Digest Books, Cincinnati, 1981

Macdonald, Ross, *On Crime Writing*, 1973

Noble, William, *Conflict, Action and Suspense*, Writer's Digest Books, Cincinnati, 1994

O'Hara, Charles E., *Fundamentals of Criminal Investigations*, CC Thomas, 1981

Porter, Dorothy, *The Monkey's Mask*, Hyland House, Melbourne, 1994

Rendell, Ruth, *An Unkindness of Ravens*, Hutchinson, London, 1985

Simpson, Helen 'Flesh and Grass' in *Unguarded Hours*, two novellas by Ruth Rendell and Helen Simpson, Pandora Press, London, 1990

Stine, Kate (ed.), *The Armchair Detective Book of Lists*, Otto Penzler Books, New York, 1995

Treat, Lawrence, *Mystery Writer's Handbook*, Writer's Digest Books, Cincinnati, 1976

Vogler, Christopher, *The Writer's Journey: Mythic Structures for Storytellers and Screenwriters*, Michael Wiese Productions, Studio City, California, 1992

Wilson, Keith D., *Cause of Death: A Writer's Guide to Death, Murder and Forensic Medicine*, Writer's Digest Books, Cincinnati, 1992

Wright, Steve, 'Winston Goes Straight' in *More Crimes for a Summer Christmas*, Allen & Unwin, Sydney, 1991